THE WRATH OF FATE

BY
ROBERT H. BROWN

ILLUSTRATED BY
JUAN PABLO VALDECANTOS ANFUSO

Book I

Prologue _____ 9

First Motion _____ 10

The Chronofax _____ 14

An Ill-Fated Vessel _____ 26

Skepticism _____ 32

Impact _____ 36

Introductions _____ 42

Scavenger Hunt _____ 54

Grease _____ 58

The Best Gimmick Ever _____ 64

Viral Piracy _____ 70

New Plans _____ 84

The Battle Of Arcot _____ 90

What the Hell Was That? _____ 102

A Stolen Monster _____ 110

Entropy _____ 124

Book II

The End Of Days _____ 136

Airship Pirates _____ 150

A Minor Redemption _____ 162

High Tortuga _____ 170

Automaton _____ 186

Reunions _____ 194

The Change Cage _____ 208

Beautiful Decline _____ 230

The Emperor's Wives _____ 244

The Wrath Of Fate _____ 254

BOOK I

Show me a man who grew up with a happy childhood, no blood or broken glass in his youth, and I will show you a man who likely has nothing to contribute to society. The same wounds that can turn a man into a villain, might instead turn him into a hero, an artist, or a leader.

Scars add character.

The history of mankind is like that, too. If you could go back in time and erase the wounds, take away the Holocaust, take away slavery, take away every time two cultures were forced to blend, take away every time something so horrible occurred that it forced the rules to change–forced people to change–if you could take away the pain of history, mankind would not be as strong as it is today.

... for better or for worse.

FIRST MOTION

There are moors just south of the ancient and tiny town of Whitby, England. Greenish-brown grass on rolling hills so steep that from the top of a hill you cannot see the bottom of the valley around it, and from the bottom of the valley all you can see is the sides of the hill but not what is on top of them.

At the top of one of these hills stood a tall wooden platform. At twenty feet high it was almost a tower, freshly built of raw unadorned lumber. Standing on top of this was a man, gray bearded and balding, wearing a herringbone coat with a fur collar. His eyes sparkled with excitement and mischief. In them you could see a nine-year-old boy, breaking some very important rules just for the sake of breaking them. Also behind those eyes was an egotistical man who knew without a doubt that there was no one within a hundred miles who could understand what he was up to, even if he had stopped to explain it to them, which he certainly would not have. Protruding from his pockets was a collection of slide rules, broken pencils and little rolls of paper, upon which there were little sketches and equations. He had a fresh cut on his right hand that was bleeding a little but he would not notice this until he sat down to lunch, if he even remembered to have lunch. Around the edges of the platform were a series of glass orbs, and inside each was a coil of copper wire wound around a ceramic spindle. Each glass ball was also attached to the others by a series of thick copper pipes, which fed into a large machine on the edge of the platform. The machine was covered with gauges and dials, along with one very large throw switch – the kind you would see in Dr. Frankenstein's laboratory. There was a small cage filled with a half dozen rabbits. The old man pulled up the sleeve of one arm, and reached into the cage. Grabbing a rabbit by the scruff of its neck, he gently lifted it out of the cage, and limped to the center of the platform (he normally walked with a cane, but today he had mistakenly left it at the bottom of the tower). He set the rabbit on top of a pile of carrots, before hobbling back to the machine at the edge of the platform.

Making sure he was outside the circle of globes, he took a deep breath and threw the switch. His eyes flickered down the now trembling pipes and rested on one of the glass orbs. It quickly filled with a glowing pink gas that swirled slowly, glowing the color of sky during a lightning storm. The rabbit flinched. Suddenly, a gust of wind blew on its fur like a tornado, the rabbit's eyes widened in surprise, and it was gone. So were the carrots and the center of the wooden platform, gone as if they had been cleanly sliced right out of the tower in a perfect circle. The tower creaked a bit, adjusting to its new weight, and lack of rigidity.

"Oops. That was unexpected," the man murmured to himself, as he clenched the railing for support.

He was a man of science, but his passion was not for learning. It was for building. Long hours of research held no joy–this was simply a means to an end. He would take his knowledge and run towards his creations with it–sometimes literally. Even upon finishing one project, he didn't rest, as he was always in a hurry to achieve his next creation.

The end result was that he sometimes overlooked very important details. In this case, his experimen left him on a nearly collapsing tower twenty feet above the ground. This hardly mattered to him at the time of his calculations. The goal was the bunny.

He pulled a golden watch from his pocket, and pushed a button on it. Exhaling impatiently, he sat down on the platform and pulled out a sandwich wrapped in waxed paper. As he took the first bite, he noticed the cut on his hand. He looked at the cut, and wondered where he had gotten it.

Presently, he saw a boy running up the hill. The boy was wearing a vest, knickerbockers and page-boy cap, and was waving a letter in the air. This letter was an invitation to meet with financiers regarding his experiment today. In his haste the old man had already reported his success to them, and now he was going to get funding to turn this little test into something much grander.

Behind the boy, in the mid-air above the center of the valley due west, at the exact height of the platform on which the doctor stood, with a puff of wind a tiny cloud formed, then quickly dissipated, revealing a circle of wood. On it was the pile of carrots and on top of that – one white rabbit.

Wood, carrots and rabbit hovered in the air for just a moment, and then gently fell out of sight to the valley below.

THE CHRONOFAX

When my father sold our family home, I was told I could go back for one last visit before the new owners took possession. The house was filled with stacks of boxes, and furniture covered in white sheets. As I walked from room to room, the sheets gave the place a spectral feel. Chairs and tables were now merely the spirits of what was once my childhood playroom, family room, and dining room. My father's workshop, where once we built toys, was now a series of empty tables. The music room was just tile, dust, and darkness.

Now that I am many years older than that young troubled version of myself, exploring the ruins of my childhood home, I can't blame my parents for running away from our family. I had an older brother named Samuel, and he had...issues. When he was six, he was so strong-willed he would terrify his babysitters, and they would run from the house. When he was ten, he fought with my parents, screaming at them, and they would scream back at him like he was an adult. When he was sixteen, he chased my mother around the house with knives from the kitchen. When he was eighteen, I was forced to lock myself in my bedroom to get away from him, and he took an axe and chopped through my door. I escaped through a window, and found my way to my grandmother's house, where I stayed for days until my parents' return. He was a monster, and my parents told no one about him, because they somehow blamed themselves for his disorders. My parents' guilt became his validation, and our family's destruction.

This left the younger children constantly in an emotional dichotomy. We hid because we didn't want to be noticed by Samuel, for fear he'd lock us out of the house or hurt us. At the same time, we wanted love and attention from mother and father that we couldn't get because they were always dealing with Samuel. If there was a conflict between one of us and him, my parents would unfairly weigh the scales of justice. "You should have known not to make him mad, this is Samuel!" They would say, as if the great crime was that we didn't cower to him soon enough. We should have known better. My parents feared him as much as we did.

This is where my pain comes from. This is the source of my hunger to be important, to be noticed, to be a hero, and not the wounded little boy. As I became older and stronger, I tried to stand up to him, to protect my sister and my mother. I wanted to be their hero, but standing up to him made *me* the villain, since *I should have known better than to stand up to Samuel.* As I walked through this dead home, this shell of a broken family, I felt a mix of fear and hatred towards those memories.

But not everything about my childhood was dark and horrific. As I entered my parents' private office, I noticed it hadn't been touched in years. The office walls were bookcases, and were still filled with hundreds of dusty old books on anthropology and psychology, some of which had been written by my parents. Masks, headdresses and weapons from various tribal peoples lined the tops of bookshelves collecting dust. Models of the human brain sat on the massive oak desk. My parents had grand careers which I believed I could never measure up to.

Maps, prickly with the pins of a hundred expeditions, lined the walls. These expeditions were no mere family vacations: this was the field research of my mother. India, Thailand, China. I made forts of coconut fronds on Polynesian sands when I was four. I played in ruined temples in the jungle when I was eight. I lived in houses made of sticks, built on stilts over elephant paddocks in the jungles of Thailand when I was sixteen.

When we traveled, I rarely saw my brother Samuel, and life was good. Samuel would be put into a boarding school, or left behind with my father often enough that I saw travel as the perfect life. It was the only time I had a happy childhood.

On the old oak desk, I found a photo of myself at age five, climbing the steps of beautiful ruins in Delhi, India. Next to it was a photo of me in Bangkok on my old rented motorcycle, a young man of fifteen, with a beautiful girl's arms wrapped around my waist. I remember racing gas-powered rickshaws in the crowded streets, and although I don't remember the girl's name anymore, I still miss the motorcycle terribly.

As I looked over all the aging artifacts, I thought, *This was my childhood.* The life of an explorer, as exciting and romantic as anyone could hope for – as long as my parents' marriage held together, and as long as we were traveling.

But now that my family had ended, so had the adventure. I had been living on my own long enough to feel like a complete failure. I had a series of lame jobs. I bagged groceries at Safeway. I sold clothes at the mall. I was even the only employee at an umbrella store. These were miserable, degrading wastes of time compared to the illustrious careers of my parents.

I hated my life, and I hated how I had turned out as much as I hated the violence of my childhood.

My only remaining dream was music. Music was part of my mother's family. My Grandma owned a music store, and my uncles were musicians playing in bands with their children. Music, to me, was the symbol of loving family, and I was good at it. I wrote music and song lyrics constantly. I dreamed of making this my life. I was often reminded by my parents that this was a pipe-dream, but it took me away from the misery of not living up to their achievements.

I started a band, and we would play on the weekends whenever we could find the time or energy away from our life-sucking day jobs. I passed through my twenties, slowly starting to hate my life, as my prospects of becoming a rock star seemed less and less likely, and my dream of returning to being an adventurer was so far gone that just remembering I had once had the dream was heart-wrenching.

Being young, money was always a worry. Bill collectors calling, a constant threat of losing my horrible apartment, always wondering how I could pay the next month's bills. I never had the hope I could climb above it all.

So here I stood, in this empty house, at the source of all my pain, but also the source of all my longing and unfulfilled dreams, looking for...*something.* Here in the dark, between African masks with horrific expressions of pain and anger, between primitive weapons both deadly and rotting, between vacant headdresses of long dead chieftains, I found something. On a small table, hand carved with the faces of gods of old, sat the Chronofax.

The Chronofax had been in my family's possession for years. It was a vintage novelty my father had purchased in London on the way back from one of our many expeditions. As far as my family was concerned, it was a one-hundred-year-old joke, like the sewn together 'mermaid mummies' you might see in a curiosity shop.

It looked like an antique typewriter, with a small greenish screen on the top that had the same sort of look as a Magic 8-Ball window. Its keys were round and laid out similarly to a contemporary keyboard. Just above the keys was an abacus-like slider, with dates on it. If I typed on the keyboard my words would appear on the screen. Then, if I pulled the lever on the side it would make a *"shunk-chiing!"* sound, and the words would disappear.

Supposedly, this machine would send a message forward in time, reappearing at whatever time was chosen. It worked, however, by clockwork, not magic. It would simply delay your message, and show it in the future. *Time Traveling letters! Magic!*

When I was a small boy, I would type letters to myself to be read when I was an adult. The letters I sent were mostly warnings. I sent them to appear in twenty years, when I could obviously use the wisdom of an eight-year-old child. I think we could all use the wisdom of an eight-year-old child at times. I would pull the lever and the note would disappear. Then I would picture some adult reading it "in the future." Part of me must have known this was futile, but I had few friends, so talking to myself at least felt like company.

So here I sat, as a young adult, before this Victorian wonder, this copper and brass magical marvel of horology. It was covered in old passports, travel journals, and a thick layer of dust, but under all the clutter, I could see the screen still glowed green.

I brushed off the old passports and maps, and wiped the dust off its screen with my sleeve. There was a letter! *Probably the last thing I had typed on it as a child*, I reassured myself. So I pulled up my father's massive old riveted leather office chair and read:

> *Dear Mr. Brown,*
>
> *One day I'll be you, so I thought I should write to you and make sure you don't change too much, or become anyone we'd hate.*
>
> *Being a kid sucks. There has been a lot of fighting and yelling lately. It's not fun here. I'm scared all the time. I can't WAIT to grow up and get out of here.*

Please please please do something cool as an adult. I need something to look forward to. Be an astronaut, or a pirate or something cool like that. Don't be a loser with a lame job at a bank or something.

If you are reading this please reply and tell me what we are when we grow up. I need something to look forward to.

~ Robbie

Well, I guess the machine did work! Some desperate message from my eight-year-old self had reappeared, and I was reading it as an adult. The message stung, especially since life was not cool or glamorous. Here was proof that as a small boy I was hoping life would get better. It hadn't, and it would get much worse for that small desperate boy. I felt like I had had the floor ripped out from under me.

Had I ever felt happy and secure? What would I say to this child, if I could respond? I worked a job I hated. After years of working for someone else, building someone else's dreams for them alone to enjoy, I had elevated myself to the position of *guy who sits in a cubicle doing something with a computer*. At least, that is the best way I could describe it to my eight-year-old self.

I angrily typed a reply. I did not think for a moment it would actually go back in time, but I just could not let that little boy have the last word, summing up my failures and fears so succinctly. It was really just me venting in the first way that came to me:

Dear Little Boy,

I'm doing my best up here, but it's REALLY hard. I have to pay ALL these bills that I never make enough money to pay. I have to buy clothes I hate, so I can wear them to a job I hate, and I have to buy gas to keep my car running while I fight gridlock on the way to the job I hate. I even have to pay for parking at the job! All of these things add up to more money than I make, which means I now owe banks money for buying things (like lame cars) that I had to buy, just to go to the job so I could try to earn the money to give to the banks!

Being an Astronaut is silly, there are like maybe ten in the whole world. Being a pirate is dangerous, and illegal, and cruel, and it does NOT mean you have a cool old pirate ship, and a sword – pirates are not really like that anymore.

No, I am not something cool, I'm just doing my best to stay afloat, but I'm slowly sinking, and it sucks, and although you hate your home and family, I miss my childhood!

-   Robert Brown

I was pissed, bitter, sad, my eyes stung, and were filling with tears. I pulled the lever and the words vanished. Then I felt a tinge of guilt: how depressed would any little boy get if he received *that*?

The screen was black now. I supposed the machine turned off, so I stood up to walk out. This whole exchange had left me angry and depressed. I walked to the door, and stood there a second asking myself if I was going to regret walking away from all these memories. Then I heard a *"shunk-chiing!"*

Instantly a shiver raced down my spine. I turned and saw that a new note had appeared on the screen! I walked quickly back and sat down again. The note read:

Dear Mr. Brown,

That can't be what life is like! It doesn't make any

sense! You're lying! You suck!

Why would you work a job you hated, so that you could only barely afford to live a life you hate?! Adventures are free! Indiana Jones never even had a wallet that I saw!

I would NEVER live the life you're describing! There is no way I would let that happen to me after so much bad has already happened.

You lie and I hate you.

- Robbie

My eyes widened, and my mind raced, *Wait a second, I think I might remember this! Didn't I get a couple of messages from this machine when I was a kid? I told dad, and he took me to talk with a guy at his work, who asked me a lot of questions about my parents' impending divorce, and if my father hit me. Dad told me not to talk about Samuel.*

The screen glowed green, waiting for a response, but this time it scared me. I didn't believe this was happening, yet at the same time I was red-faced, angry and sad. I hated myself, and I wondered if all those deeply scarring emotions had led me to invent that this had all happened.

The screen glowed green, waiting for a reply.

I sat quietly for more than an hour, replaying memories from my childhood, wondering when my life had gotten on this horrible track, and how much longer I was going to stay on it. I didn't believe my dreams were remotely possible any more. I couldn't remember anything I still enjoyed, or if I had any dreams left.

I had nothing positive to tell this little boy, but I was not going to hurt him again. I would not respond until I had better news, and that meant I had to make better news happen.

This reminded me of my band, the only dream left. The band had just been forced to turn down a great festival eight hundred miles away, because we couldn't afford to get there, and we couldn't take the time off work required for the drive. We had even been offered two decent slots. I was tired of making excuses and hiding from life. I reached into my pocket, and pulled out my phone.

"Look, it's not just about the day job thing. Hold on, I'm gonna three-way call Kristina and Traci, they need to be in on this," Krzysztof said. He was our bass player, and a damned good one, but his investment in the band was not huge. He and his wife Traci had their own band prior to this one. They only set it aside to join my band, so "someone else could handle the bullshit." It might seem glamorous, but running a band is not easy.

"Hello?" Kristina answered. Kristina is my wife. Well, recently my wife, although she had been my keyboard player and friend since she was a teenager.

"Hey, Kristina, this is Krzysztof, and I've got Robert on the line. We are talking about the shows in Salt Lake City."

"I thought we had decided we couldn't play those." Kristina replied.

"Well, Robert thinks we should..." Krzysztof started to say before I interrupted.

"Hey, it's me," I said "I'm sorry, but I had a change of heart. I think we have to stop saying no to everything that isn't completely comfortable. We are saying no to nineteen out of twenty shows. All we end up playing is the same bar in Seattle over and over again," I said. "We can't make new fans by playing to the same fans over and over." What I wasn't saying was, *we can't give up our tiny lives for something better if we aren't willing to work harder at it. You have to do more to get more!* I knew everybody else had stopped trying for something more, years ago, seduced by the comfortable placation of a nine-to-five job. However, my recent letter from myself had reinvigorated my discontent.

"We just played Chicago," said Traci, who had joined the call.

"That was a year and a half ago!" I snapped back, trying not to sound desperate, and regretting the speed at which I retorted.

"Sixteen months. Don't exaggerate," Krzysztof said, defending Traci. "You always exaggerate everything," Things were starting to heat up a little.

"I wasn't exaggerating, I was rounding up. At this rate, we're talking about one show every two years! How are we supposed to get anywhere with only one show every two years!?!"

I think they could hear the desperation in my voice, and Kristina came in with a sympathetic tone. "Aw, honey, you are somewhere now! We don't need to be big rock stars to be proud of ourselves." She was trying to make me feel better, but this wasn't working with me. In fact, it was making things worse. Compromising my self-definition felt like the last step before I submitted to having a mediocre life. "Besides, we are going to lose money on the shows! The plane tickets will cost more than they are offering to pay us. We can't *afford* to play the shows!" This band was getting too spoiled with their daily incomes to do the 'play for free' gigs anymore.

Then I had an idea. "If I can get us to the shows for free, will you do it?"

"How?" Everyone asked at almost the same time.

"Leave that to me, I know a guy that can help."

We hung up, and I turned back to the Chronofax, ready to type. Then I stopped, and I thought, *No, I'll respond when I have something better to report.*

AN ILL-FATED VESSEL

Some years after we last saw him, the old man in the herringbone coat sat on the bucking bench seat of a 1903 Knox: a turn-of-the-century flatbed truck normally used for delivering produce. Alongside him sat the driver in a page-boy cap and goggles. The driver's scarf kept brushing the old man's face. This happened with almost enough frequency to change his mood, from one of excitement to one of annoyance.

The Knox was the first in a line of trucks. There were eight trucks in all, and their flat open beds were piled high with wooden crates. Jutting from the tops of these were copper pipes and massive, straw-packed glass orbs. The trucks wound their way around the streets of London toward the shipyards.

They arrived at a newly constructed wall and gate, large enough to completely hide the dock from the view of anyone walking on the street. Standing by the gate were four sailors of unequal size, poorly shaven, tanned to the color of old leather, and uncomfortable in their ill-fitting uniforms.

Noticing the man in the herringbone coat, the largest of them spoke, "Piss off, you! You've got the wrong address. You can't bring your groceries down here!"

"I am Doctor Calgori. I believe your captain is waiting for me," said the old man, standing up in his seat.

"Oi, we do knows you! We knows him!" said the smallest of the sailors, while elbowing the largest. "Lemme fetch the captain, and we'll see what he wants us to do with yoose." With that, he slipped through the gate.

The largest of the sailors then stepped around toward the side of the first truck and tipped one of the crates precariously, so he could see inside it. "Is this where you've got your magical contraptions, Doctor? 'Ow's about giving us a little magic whiles we waits?"

Doctor Calgori scrambled clumsily out of the truck, "Careful with that, my good man! It is not magic. Those orbs are both delicate and expensive! I have no idea where we could acquire another on such short notice! I had them specially made to my exact specifications, and lacking even one would unbalance the..."

At this point an orb rolled out of the box and popped like a giant light bulb at the feet of the sailor. As it burst, the pink gas that was inside it formed a small cloud just two feet off the ground, surrounding the sailor's waist. The cloud began to rain, and a tiny bolt of lightning cracked like a whip, striking the sailor in the knee. In his fright, he leapt backward into the chest of his enraged captain, who had walked quietly up during the commotion, and watched the whole scene unfold without uttering a word.

"Buffoon!" the captain exclaimed with a look of disgust on his face. He swung his cane and struck the sailor in his left eye. The brass T-shaped cane handle sunk deeply into the sailor's eye socket. The captain then removed it, with both difficulty and disgust.

"You cretin!" he continued to roar, even as the stricken sailor fell to his knees in pain, grasping his face. "I don't know whether to call you a liability, or a Punchinello! This equipment is worth more than your life!" He raised his cane again to strike.

"Good sir!" cried Doctor Calgori. "That is more than excessive!"

The captain lowered his cane, and glared angrily back at Calgori. He glared for just a second, but then his demeanor flickered to one of cordial politeness. "Ah, Doctor Calgori! I was told you had arrived! I'm Captain Brussel. I hope you didn't find your journey too taxing?"

"Not at all," Calgori answered, not masking his distaste. With a concerned look, he walked over to check on the sailor on the ground.

"Pay no mind to this mongrel, he's made of stern stuff. I'm sure he's learnt his lesson, and will be back at his post in no time. Isn't that right, mongrel?" Though he was shaking, the sailor on the ground did not utter a reply. The captain continued, "Now, let me show you what we have prepared for you."

"I will admit I am curious as to why we are at the docks." Doctor Calgori said shakily, as the Captain led him away from the wounded sailor. This cruel violence wasn't the first the Doctor had seen in his life, but it was jarring nonetheless.

Through the gates was a beehive of commotion, as dozens of men labored around a massive sailing ship. The ship's design was easily a hundred years out of date. It was vintage, even for the early 1900s. Yet its construction was new, even unfinished in places. The ship looked like a gorgeous and ornate vessel from the height of the Age of Sail: intricately carved wood, cannon, ropes, masts, sails, and figurehead. It was majestic and beautiful, and completely new. It was a strong contrast to the beaten and scarred sailors who were busy loading or rigging her. They filled the air with the smell of their sweat, and with startling profanity.

"Why have you brought me to this...pirate's ship?" the Doctor asked in distaste for sailors and vessel. Calgori had been through a lot, and at this age his memory was very selective, as you will see.

"This is the vessel you are to fit with your...contraptions." the captain said. Calgori's eyes narrowed as he squinted at the boat, but the captain continued, "I realize she looks old-fashioned, but I assure you she's very new, and beautifully built. A great deal of consideration was put into her construction, and her looks were very much part of the grand plan.

"Though she looks heavy and antiquated, she is as light and modern as 1906 can produce. This is the *H.M.S. Ophelia.* It's a Shakespearean reference, you see, and a bloody good joke as Ophelia floated herself, didn't she?" The captain ended with a perverse chuckle.

The Doctor glared at the grinning captain. "Hamlet's Ophelia died in the water, as will you and your crew! Do you have any idea what that hull will go through when we attempt to travel, if it's submerged in water?!"

"I'm sure you have your work cut out for you, and I would hope you are capable of making the necessary modifications?" This question was almost a dare, and Calgori wondered if he saw a threat behind the captain's bushy eyebrows.

"Quite," said Calgori, and he paused while he made some calculations in his head. "However, your men up on those masts are wasting their time. Bring them down, and fetch me some porters. This will completely change the schedule I originally proposed. We will need to unpack and, I think, we will need to order canvas."

"We have two complete sets of sails, Doctor."'

"It is not for the sails. I shall make you a list of new supplies. Your superiors really should have spoken to me before they commissioned the ship's construction. They completely misunderstood my quite specific directions. I am sure it fits *your* plans, but it is completely unsuitable for mine. Unless you are planning to die on your first trip, we have a lot of modifications to make, not the least being that we need to get this boat *out of the water!*"

As the Doctor was escorted aboard, the sailors from the gate shouldered their wounded friend up the gang plank, and tried to hush his mumbled threats. "None of that talk now, mongrel. You've got no option but to serve your captain or go back to prison."

"We'll see," said the sailor. "We'll bloody well see."

SKEPTICISM

"Do you know how many bands have died in small plane crashes?" Kristina asked from the back seat of our green Ford Windstar minivan. The paint was peeling on the hood, and it was hot and sticky inside with the sweat of the five young musicians. We had less than one day to travel from Gig Harbor, Washington, to the music festival we were to play in Salt Lake City, Utah.

"Just because it's happened before, doesn't mean it'll happen to us. We'll be fine," I answered. Many times during my life I felt like I was forcing the musicians of my band, against their will, into doing something that would make their lives bearable. They all complained about their jobs, yet every step of progress the band made, no matter how small, seemed a step uphill. It was as if I couldn't get them to see there was something outside their little lives, and so they constantly pulled against me.

"Sure beats the hell out of driving the whole way to there in this damned minivan. This thing smells like old sandwiches," grumbled our bass player, only half-jokingly. He was a small guy, dyed black hair, unshaven, with a little tuft of facial hair under his bottom lip. His style of humor was to complain in a funny voice so it sounded like he was impersonating a grouchy old man, all while really voicing a complaint. It was effective, since you couldn't argue with a "joke," but it was really just his way of bitching about everything. "If we drive now, by the time we'd get to the gig in Salt Lake City, we'll all smell like old sandwiches!"

"Patsy Cline. They had to ID her body from a piece of her the size of a loaf of bread. That was all that was left of her." Kristina was sort of our – not voice of reason – but voice of perpetual doubt, despite all reason. Or at least that is how she was in those days. She was a tall blonde, and was usually seen with pigtails. She was also the type of pianist that would stay up late reading biographies of long-dead composers through the reading glasses she did not want anyone to know she wore.

"We'll be fine. Statistically speaking, there is a greater chance of dying in the shower than dying in a plane crash," I said from behind the wheel. Thank God we were not going to drive all the way to Salt Lake City. If people were going to bitch the whole time, I think I would have cracked before we got there.

"John Denver."

"Look, if we were gonna drive we would have had to have left five hours ago. We *have* to fly now!" I retorted. I'm the lead singer of this band, I write the songs, (mostly about how much life sucks, or about my parents' divorce) as well as make the website, newsletters, etc. In those days, we were the kind of band that stood onstage wearing all black, trying hard not to smile, even though we were really excited that all of seventy-five people turned out for the show.

"Buddy Holly."

Our odorific van pulled off the back road, onto the gravel of a local airfield. A few weeks ago at an after-party one of our fans bragged about his pilot's license. He offered to fly us to a show if we bought gas for his plane. At the time the idea seemed exciting and glamorous, but as the dust settled in the parking lot of what had to be the smallest airport in the country, and we saw the tiny rusted plane ahead of us, I was starting to think that Kristina might be right. On the other hand, this *was* starting to look like an adventure.

SKEPTICISM

IMPACT

Within a couple of hours we were bucking around through deep purple clouds somewhere over Idaho. Rain was pelting the plane's windshield so hard that we had to shout at one another to be heard. After a while it was not worth the effort. The only one who still had anything to say was Kristina.

"Lynyrd Skynyrd!"

Suddenly, there was a clearing in the clouds. In front of us was something unexplainable: a huge black silhouette the shape of a massive football, so large it filled the front windows.

The massive shape was wider than it was tall, and we were not entirely sure how far off the ground we were, so the pilot tried to climb in the vain hope of going over it. He jerked back on the control yoke, assuming the plane would leap up as well. But the plane was small, the weather was fierce, and the plane had no noticeable response other than violent shaking. The passengers in the plane now screamed in fear, and the pilot looked frantic.

The dark silhouette was too big, our plane was too poorly powered, and the pilot was outwitted by a lack of response from his controls. Soon the shadow filled our view, and the last thing I remember was the dashboard of our plane crushing the pilot and his chair into my legs.

When I woke I was disoriented, cold, wet. There was blood on my face and a crushing pain in my legs where they were pinned by the pilot's seat in front of me. From my viewpoint, our plane was precariously squished to the side of a cliff. The tail of the plane was missing. It had broken off just behind Kristina's and my seat, and rest of the band was nowhere to be seen. In times like these people tend to shut down parts of their brain so they can deal with the task at hand. I did this now, ignoring my missing bandmates and burying all the emotional trauma to deal with later.

I looked through the broken windshield. Impossibly, the cliff seemed to be made of canvas! There was no going out through the windshield. That way was blocked by the wet fabric "cliff." The right window of the cockpit was shattered but still intact, and the combination of the pelting rain and the spiderweb of cracks in the glass made it impossible to see through. Our only escape route was through the missing left side window.

I saw a rope ladder just within reach of the window. In fact, our entire plane seemed to be hanging from rope ladders. They started above us, dropping into the black abyss below. This left us with a tricky decision, climb up to where the ladder stayed close to the cliff, which seemed to level off, or climb down to where the rope ladder dangled over the black abyss.

Finally, and after a little discussion in the raging rain, Kristina and I decided that going down was best. This accursed trip was not going to be over until we got "down" from wherever we were so, after a few minutes of struggling to push what was left of the pilot out of our way, down we went.

As we descended, the ladder separated from the side of the "cliff," and we came to the most baffling scene yet. There was a sailing ship hanging from hundreds of massive ropes in the blackness of the sky. It was made of ornately carved wood, like a classic pirate ship. Copper and brass machinery protruded from huge sections of it, as well as giant glass orbs filled with swirling pink gas that glowed dimly. Networks of glass and copper tubes occasionally shot little lighted capsules through them. At least a dozen weathered figures in long oiled raincoats, leather helmets and massive goggles ran on deck, climbing the ropes in a general panic, looking like enraged ants when you step on their hill.

We clambered over the railing, and I noticed Kristina was shivering. Not from fear, mind you, but from the icy cold, wet, and pure exhaustion of the day's misadventure. I hoisted her with one arm and, unnoticed by the crew, we headed for a large door in the aft of the ship.

Swinging open the door, we found that it led to one of the most beautifully furnished living rooms I have ever been in. Deep leather sofas, chandeliers dangling as the ship swung on its ropes, edged tables filled with glass bottles of all shapes and sizes – some had fallen and smashed on the floor. A massive wingback chair lay overturned just behind a huge brass captain's wheel, and what I guessed was a periscope showed the view out the front of the ship.

Suspended from the ceiling was a very detailed model of what looked like a pirate ship hanging under a zeppelin. The pirate ship was bristling with cannon, surrounded with miniature glass orbs and tubes. Could this be where we stood now: on a flying ship, hanging under a massive zeppelin, some Victorian-era airship? This certainly accounted for what we had seen so far. I could see the "canvas cliff" rope ladder we had descended, and the railing we climbed over, and the deck we stumbled across, all in miniature.

The far wall of this room was fitted with ornate stained-glass panels. Gorgeous deep reds, greens and teals, with gilded leading, cut to depict different nautical and aeronautical themes. Just outside the windows, two massive propellers could be seen spinning furiously, and there was a man-sized hole in the glass wall just behind the captain's overturned chair. Near the hole stood two silhouettes engaged in somber debate, looking quite distressed.

"Well, he was sitting right in his chair, wasn't he?" asked the taller silhouette. I would later learn his name was Jean-Paul. Jean-Paul was Creole: huge, black, bald, and intimidating, if you didn't know him. When you got to know him, you knew he was quiet, kind, and always genteelly cheerful. He wore silk harem pants and a mandarin jacket which made him look like a cross between a genie and a South Seas pirate.

"Where is he now? Did he fall through the glass?" asked the silhouette next to him, pointing to the hole in the window. This was Tanner. He wore a plain black bowler, huge boots that came nearly to his knees, and a ragged vest which might at one time have been an army field jacket. Completing his attire was a kilt.

"Yes! It looks like he went right through the window. You'd better tell Daniel what's happened, and possibly Calgori." Jean-Paul then turned to leave, and as he did he saw us. "Who are you?"

"I'm Robert, this is Kristina. We are really sorry to be here, but I'm afraid we..." as I was speaking, the man with the bowler turned, slipped and fell to the floor. As he tried to get up, he slipped again. When he looked at his hands they were covered with blood, as was the floor around him.

INTRODUCTIONS

We were taken to a small cabin, and given some odd-looking clothes; hand-stitched, dark colors, military but formally cut – not like the baggy fitting chamois of today's armies. As we sat on the edge of small bunks under itchy, stiff blankets, we were given cups of hot, incredibly strong, bitter tea.

For the first hour, we said nothing. None of it seemed possible, and none of it seemed good. I shivered under my blanket worried that Kristina was under her blanket blaming me for everything that had gone wrong. Blaming me for the crash she warned me about, blaming me for the death of our band-mates, our friends. I feared her opinions of me so much, I didn't dare start the conversation, so I sat as silent as she.

I felt deep, dark self-loathingly horrible. If only I could take it back, redo the day in a way that didn't end like this. But is that what I really wanted? Part of me was screaming, "See, you're not supposed to leave that life of reliable employment." While another quieter part was whispering excitedly, "This is better, you're traveling again! You're off the grid, and on an adventure! This is where you are supposed to be."

That night, a meeting was called to assess damage and form a plan. Kristina and I were invited, since the crew seemed to feel we could add something to the conversation. It turned out they *needed* us.

We were led down dark wooden corridors, past many round portholes, and through large double doors. The less expendable members of the crew were assembled in the map room, which was a very long narrow room with no maps at all. In the center of it was a massive and very complex slide rule, about fifteen feet long, with dozens of shifting scales (the parts of a slide rule that slide). Above this, and in full motion, was a beautiful brass, copper, and pewter orrery.

Let me explain: if a globe is a three dimensional map of the Earth, then think of an orrery as a three-dimensional map of the solar system. This one was not only in motion, but you could increase or decrease its speed, or reverse its motion using one of the scales of the slide rule in the center of the room.

Another machine about the size of a school desk sat at one end of the room. It was connected both to the orrie and the glass orbs around the ship. The machine was covered with gauges, dials and one very large throw switch, just the kind you might see in Dr. Frankenstein's laboratory.

The excitement of this scene was pushing the dark feelings of guilt from my mind. It was only a temporary distraction, but one that was welcomed nonetheless.

Tanner was speaking as we entered, "I really don't think we can ask any more of Dr. Calgori while he's in his present state. He's very ill, and I don't think we should disturb him."

"Well, he's not in command," said a tall, slender, and very "proper military" man. "I'm not sure he could help us much anyway. He seems as lost as we are. I had been trying to get our orders out of the Captain over the last few days, but the plans were not forthcoming. And now the captain is lost. I don't suppose it would make sense to declare him dead, but he's certainly not onboard. It would appear in the collision he was knocked from his chair, and fell through the window of his cabin."

"He didn't tell you the 'plan,' Daniel, because he 'ad no plan! Capt'n was stumped!" said a third, whiskery man with a fresh eye patch that he occasionally mopped under with a rag. I was beginning to notice that most of the crew in the room was filthy, wet, and very battered. They obviously had not been having an easy time of things.

Kristina and I had been sitting quietly listening to all of this. Although I felt unexpectedly at home in this strangely ornate and luxurious environment, I'm sure I looked quite out of place, so I kept my mouth shut. At this point it became apparent that nobody here was any more "in their element" then I was. "What exactly is the problem?" I asked.

There was a long pause as it seemed people were working out just how to begin, or who I was, or who was to fill me in on what was going on.

Finally Daniel answered, "You are aboard the *HMS Ophelia*, an experimental vessel designed in 1897 by Dr. Calgori for Her Majesty's Fleet. It's a time-traveling vessel. The good Doctor's experiment was funded by the British Empire with the direct goal of correcting the outcome of any historical battle the crown viewed as a failure. When fully functional, our mission will be to travel back in time, and turn the tides of previous military failures to the favor of the English crown. This journey you've caught us on was our maiden voyage – it was a test run that seems to have gone awry. We left port on January 8th, 1906, and arrived here two hours later."

"1906. You're from 1906?" I asked calmly.

Now, you might think I'm taking this a little too well. That's not the case. I have a rule in life: when someone presents me with an outrageous story, instead of arguing with them, I let them finish their tale. After I've heard their whole story it's easier to decide how it affects me, and if it hurts me at all to pretend I believe them. Whether or not I actually believe them is irrelevant, and telling them so would interrupt the story. In this case, the tale was too much fun to contest. I wanted to hear the whole story, true or not. Although I wanted this to be true. Besides, the night had already been more than unusual, so this crazy tale didn't really seem that far out in left field.

"You're from 1906?" I asked again.

"Yes. Although construction was well funded, the Crown was a bit skeptical as to the ability of Dr. Calgori's contraption to *accurately* navigate through time and return. Because of this, we were not particularly well crewed. The British navy didn't want to risk anyone of value."

At this there were some protesting grunts and groans from around the room.

"The quality of your poorly articulated dissent proves my point, I think," Daniel continued in an even more authoritative voice. "Most of the crew was drafted from various prisons around the Empire, including myself. I actually am 'career military,' just not *this* military. Still, the number of trained and competent sailors is slim." At this point I noticed that Daniel's accent was not English, but American, like my own.

Tanner continued Daniel's narration, as if to smooth over what he considered too harsh a description of the crew around them, "It's a fine crew, despite anyone's prior profession. Everyone is doing their *best*."

At "doing their best" Daniel made a disapproving sound. "Anyway, this is the maiden voyage, but instead of returning to the Napoleonic wars, we seem to have found ourselves elsewhere. We have no idea where or when we are. I am hoping you have some idea."

"The year is 2006," I said. "You are flying somewhere over Utah, um, in the United States of America."

"That's not far from what we were guessing," said the shaky voice of an old man who was just now hobbling into the room. He was leaning heavily on an ornately carved cane, and the room became reverently silent as he entered. "Although I'm a little surprised that this is only ninety-eight years in the future."

He was old, and frail, and somewhere behind his eyes was a sadness, as infinitely deep as water falling off the edge of a flat world. When he saw me, he startled, far more than anyone should at merely seeing a stranger on board. *Is it my punk rock hair?* I thought, but that didn't seem to answer his look. "Goodness, gracious!" he exclaimed. And then he chuckled. "Well, it would appear I *have* become Merlin. Welcome aboard, Wart!"

"Doctor, you shouldn't be out of bed!" Tanner said, interrupting what we all thought was a burst of Alzheimer's. It would be years before I knew what Dr. Calgori meant, but it was not Alzheimer's.

"Yes, Mum," Calgori said condescendingly. "I'll get back to bed as soon as I'm convinced you lot know what you're doing. We are rid of the captain, so in that way we are better off than when we started..." The crew was silent. No one made a sound, but one or two sailors did exchange glances.

Calgori turned back to me. "We need to refuel. The first trip had a surprising effect on our fuel supply, and I'm afraid we can't get back without refilling our tanks. Since Daniel and I were not sure how people of your time would react to us, we've been hiding in this miserable cloud until we had a better idea of where to find fuel, and how to procure it, since our money would be unlikely to still be in use now. Also, we need to make repairs. We have gaping holes in our underside, due to a mountain range we did not expect. Also, from what you are telling me it would appear I made a nearly catastrophic error in my calculations— either that, or the earth spins at an uneven rate."

"What does the rate of the earth have to do with the fact that instead of going back in time, you went forward in time one hundred years?" Daniel asked.

"Oh, *that* was no miscalculation. I had no intention of going back in time, regardless of what your people were ordering. I needed some information that I *assume* is readily available at this time, and would make the rest of our navigation simpler. After procuring that, I planned to head back to our mission."

Kristina spoke, for the first time this evening. "I don't mean to spoil the fun, but isn't time travel impossible? Didn't I read that by showing how a single photon can not travel faster than the speed of light, scientists have proven time travel is impossible?" She had a bit of her defiant and infinitely skeptical look showing from behind her bedraggled hair.

"That's nonsense," Calgori said. "All that those scientists proved is that they do not understand how it could work, not that it is impossible. Time travel is certainly possible. In fact, it's impossible *not* to time travel! Everything in existence is constantly moving forward in time. Varying the speed at which something moves through time is easy; and easily proven. If you can vary your speed enough, compared with everything else, you can go anywhen!"

"Anyway," he continued, "we left 1906 off the coast of Wales, and emerged over a mountain range which leads me to believe the earth is spinning at an uneven rate, like the weighted wheels of a train. *Voomp Voomp Voomp.*" And he made an uneven spinning motion with his hand.

The room was silent. Obviously no one had any idea what he was talking about. He sighed, "This vessel can change the time in which it exists. However, the universe is not still. Planets move, not only around the sun, but they spin as they move as well. My first efforts at time travel were effective, because I sent objects forward in time only a few minutes. They would disappear, and reappear at the time I expected, but always a few yards in the direction of the sunset. This is because the earth is constantly twisting toward the sunrise. The object would reappear exactly where it was when it had left, only the earth would be in a different position."

"When I increased the duration of time I was transporting the object, it would be further away from where it started, and sometimes either very high in the air, or buried in the ground – depending on the time of day. This is because the earth is not only spinning, but rotating around the sun as well."

Mongrel now looked a touch disgruntled. He was trying to picture this, but the thought was too big for him, and wouldn't fit in his brain. He glanced at Tanner, who was looking at the Doctor with sympathy, so he decided Dr. Calgori must be speaking nonsense. He mumbled a "Poor chap," and made a pitying frown.

Calgori responded to this with a raised eyebrow, and continued more slowly, "It became apparent that if I was to send a vessel forward in time, or backward, it would be best to do it far away from *anything*. As high in the air as possible, to avoid the possibility of it reappearing inside of a solid object. And if it was traveling more than fifteen minutes or so, it was also *crucial* that the vessel arrived precisely at the same time of year as when it departed, or else the earth would be in a different position in its orbit around the sun, and it could end up buried, or more likely, lost forever in the stars."

Every face in the room but Calgori's was now wide-eyed, open-mouthed, and horrified. It would seem that they finally understood what he was getting at. A tin cup fell from someone's hand and rattled on the floor.

"Oh, buck up, you ninnies. You're all still alive. I've got you here...now...and I will..." But at that point the doctor flushed and collapsed.

Tanner helped him to a chair and, after a brief pause, Daniel continued. "Our mission is now threefold – obtain lumber, make repairs, and possibly make design changes, since it would appear that the last-minute changes to the *Ophelia* are not as structurally sound as we had hoped. Then we need to acquire fuel, and we need food. We've been adrift up here for a couple of weeks, and I don't know how much longer it will be before we can return to London, so we need to resupply soon."

At this point I recognized why I was here. I said, "I have a proposition to make you. I think we can help with all of these, since we know *this* time vastly better than any of you. It was smart to keep your presence a secret. Governments in our time don't like anything unlicensed and free."

"Is there a time when they do?" Calgori mumbled, glowering.

"You won't be free for long," I added, "if they catch you. So you need to operate completely undetected as long as we are in this time. I can direct your acquisitions of food, fuel, and what... spare parts? In exchange for my helping you, I want to return with you back in time. We'll have to figure out when and how we do this, but at some point I'd like to try to do something that prevents our friends from dying today." I had spent the hours since the crash in a mix of emotions. Somewhere in the back of my mind was the ongoing argument: *Did I cause the death of my friends by ignoring Kristina's fears? Did I kill my friends in my own need for a less mundane life? What would I do differently, if I could do it all again?* Here I stood being told that I could in fact go back and do it all again. At least, if I stuck with this ship, and if the stars all lined up correctly.

Also, I have to admit this was no less the motivation: now,

somehow, my life had become an adventure. Scary, cold, wet and confusing, but isn't that how so many adventures begin?

Doctor Calgori wrinkled his brow at my proposal. "That's a noble cause, trying to retroactively save the lives of your friends. One we possibly can't grant. How can you, as a result of meeting us, alter time so you never crashed into us to begin with? That's an unpredictable paradox. I know quite a few Belgian Hares who would agree that 'unpredictable' is a bad thing, when it comes to moving through time." (This last comment didn't make sense until we later learned of his time travel experiments with rabbits. The Belgian Hares didn't all survive).

"It'll take some thinking," I said. "I'd rather stick with you now and hope to eventually find a way to undo their deaths rather than just walk away having known I caused their deaths and did nothing."

"Before we accept your offer, I'd like to hear how you plan to acquire these things for us," Daniel said, bringing us back to task.

"The food part is easy. All we need is money. I don't actually have any, but Kristina and I have a job...a gig. We're professional musicians. We had two shows booked this weekend. We missed the first, but could still make the second. Assuming we can find a way to still perform the show, we'll be owed about $500 for it."

"Criminy! That's a bloody fortune!"

"No, it's really not. Not anymore, but it should get us a fair share of groceries, if we keep things simple. For a crew this size I think that'll only feed us for a week or two on canned foods, and that's if we're careful. However, that's not going to be enough to get all the supplies needed to repair and fuel this ship. The problem is, most of our band is dead."

"I play a few instruments, if it would help. So does Jean-Paul," offered Tanner.

"Actually, that'd be great! We're supposed to be a five-person band. The audience and the concert promoters are expecting five people, and very specific songs and arrangements. We've only got two of our five musicians left! We need to give them what they're expecting, or we won't get paid."

Tanner was getting excited. "I'm sure we could follow along with your music!"

"All right, you can sort out your *quintet* later. Many of these sailors play music, maybe not the way you are used to, but I'm sure we can work something out for your recital tomorrow night. For now, let's lay some plans for fuel and repairs. We need wood and metal, in large quantities," said Daniel.

"...and some sort of flammable oil for the burners," Dr. Calgori interjected. "I kept the fuel specifications simple, so that we could still find something suitable if we went quite a ways backward in time," Calgori said, now slumped over in a chair, sipping black tea from a copper mug.

"Flammable oil? Would vegetable oil do?" Kristina asked. "The kind you deep-fry in? If so, I know where we might get some of that around here."

"For spare parts, I'm thinking wrecking yards and lumber yards–they should be pretty easy to spot from the air, and they keep most of their stuff outside," I offered. "We should be able to fly in at night, and just pick stuff up. Without entering a building, we won't have to worry about security systems or video cameras."

At this the rest of the crew looked blank. They had no idea what I was talking about. I had them! Without me, they were lost, and they knew it.

SCAVENGER HUNT

Somewhere in the middle of a vast deserted highway southeast of Boise, Idaho, there is an odd diametric contrast. On one side of the road is a massive home and garden store. Wealthy people (or their contractors and gardeners) drive from all over the state to buy the lumber stacked outside, or the swimming pools, the garden statues that looked as if they were from an Italian villa, or even a the Victorian-style greenhouse with real leaded-glass and wrought-iron framework.

On the other side of the road was a vast field of four hundred eighteen rotting cars, thirty-four abandoned boats, six grounded airplanes and one long dead submarine, the latter of which was mounted on a huge sign over the front gate, which read "Dave's Wrecking – used parts for anything".

At 1:18 a.m., nobody saw our sails on the horizon. At 1:26 a.m. nobody heard our propellers overhead. At 1:43 a.m. nobody saw the rope with a massive hook, and two gloved and be-goggled men being lowered from the ship. One of those two men was me, the other was Daniel.

They reeled us right into the heart of the rusting graveyard. Our boots touched earth, crunching on the mix of gravel and old washers, bolts, bottle caps, spark plugs, and flattened beer cans that made up the path between stacked vehicles. Daniel had a list of oddly described parts. It was my job to help translate the list into their modern equivalents. For example:

Item 6: a device to generate electricity from the motion of a turning axis.

Item 17: A device that creates varying degrees of forward thrust by converting electricity into the spinning of wheels.

From that I knew we were looking for a car alternator (which creates voltage from a spinning axis attached to your car motor), and a golf cart motor (which converts electricity into forward thrust). Somehow, all these parts would be repurposed by Dr. Calgori in order to fix the airship, and hopefully allow more stable travel.

Actually, the first part of this scavenger hunt was going to be tools. You can't pull the alternator out of a pale blue '74 Mustang Gia with Victorian-era tools, so our first stop was going to be the shop.

We headed by flickering lantern light over to a series of garages. The least run-down seemed the most promising, so Daniel and I lifted open the massive rolling garage door. Inside was a series of tool benches that Daniel headed towards, but I stopped, mesmerized by a vintage 1936 Chang Jiang motorcycle and side car. I had dreamed of this bike all my life, and here it stood before me, right in the middle of my big adventure.

This isn't a "fancy" bike. It's not expensive, or powerful, or luxurious. But it is exactly the kind of thing you'd see a 1940s tomb raider speed away from Nazis on. It wasn't on Dr. Calgori's list, but we were here stealing stuff, right? Typically, I wouldn't jump to stealing something so quickly, but this week we seemed to be about bending rules a bit. Context seemed to be reshaping my morality.

To be completely honest, this did start a "problem". Later that night crew helped themselves to a lot of devices and trinkets from the twenty-first century, probably following my lead. This did come in handy later on, but I'm still stunned how fast all the rules drop from your mind when your world gets a little off its beaten path. Is this what causes looters to loot? Rules of life change, so you stop following your morality? Anyway, *lets hope this isn't habit-forming.*

"Daniel, I think we will need this," I said, pointing to the motorcycle.

"That on the list?" Daniel asked.

"Not sure, but it won't hurt to have," I said.

"What is it, some sort of small wheeled, motorized Boneshaker?" he asked.

"Um. I have no idea what that is, but yes, we need it. I need it," I said.

"Okay, let's push it out to the hook," he said.

I started to push on the handle bars, and suddenly the bike growled at me. At least, that's what appeared to have happened. In truth, the bike wasn't growling, it was a large brown dog in the sidecar.

Daniel reached for the dog's collar, but the dog bared long, yellow teeth and snapped. So I tried talking lovey-dovey to it, "Eh dare, widdle doogy. Wanna get out? Out? Down! DOWN!!"

The dog laid back down into the sidecar, its head on its paws.

"Fine, we'll take the dog, too," Daniel said.

GREASE

Lilith Tess stamped furiously into the cabin, covered in engine grease from her ratted red pig-tails to her bare feet. She was smaller and younger then the rest of the crew, a fact that she reveled in, since in her mind youth, beauty, smallness, intelligence and success were all the same thing. She wore a flared, pleated skirt, and a tiny corset, which would have looked inappropriate on an adult woman's figure, but on her just-past-girlish figure it looked closer to a cheerleader uniform then lingerie. She dropped a five-pound crescent wrench on the floor, and the resounding *clang* was still echoing as she began to unbuckle the various harnesses she was wearing.

"Finished the cleaning?" I asked, not looking up from a book the Doctor had given me (a handwritten book on piloting this airship), while holding the main captain's wheel in my spare hand.

"Yeah, and I'm gonna be scrubbing bugs off my goggles for a week! Not to mention that it will take *forever* to brush out my hair," she said. "Hey, watch what you're…"

While reading, I was also holding the Captain's wheel inattentively with my other hand, and trying to wrap my head around what handle created lift, what lever tipped the nose up or down, and which throttle pushed us left and right without changing our direction. There were so many handles, chains, levers, and wheels, it could take weeks to learn. I would have been better with a keyboard and mouse, or an xBox controller. "Honestly, no one was cross-trained on this?" I asked Tanner.

Tanner quickly glanced at the newly repaired window behind where I stood, the spot where blood had been hastily cleaned from the floor, and said unconvincingly, "Um, nope," and then added in a monotone, "Thank god we have you."

"Look, this plan is lame. I don't have a damn thing to do in it!" Lilith said.

"Well, we don't need you for this one. This is a *small* plan, and it only needs a couple people," I said, wondering who this girl was, and exactly how she had become a member of the crew.

"Maybe she could hold onto the rope?" Tanner broke in. "She really should be included."

"What? Jean Paul is going to hold the rope," I was baffled. "It needs to be someone strong enough to..."

"She could do Kristina's part," Tanner volunteered, while Lilith stare at me defiantly, hands on her hips.

Still baffled, I said, "Yeah, but Kristina cooks. This plan needs someone who cooks, and Lilith doesn't...whoa!" The cabin was slowly starting to tip. The portholes along the left side were filling with pink sky and white fluffy clouds, and the on the right, hills.

"Little to the left," uttered Tanner. "And perhaps level it off as well, Captain?" He caught a shot glass just as it rolled off the bar, and stuck it in his waistcoat pocket.

"Yeah, that's just *fantastic* piloting..." Lilith jeered, and stormed out.

"I got it, I got it..." I glanced out the periscope that substituted for a front window on this lower bridge. The *Ophelia* also had a flying bridge on deck, but this was less windy, and therefore afforded easier reading. "It looks like we are nearly there anyway." I grabbed a brass handle on the ceiling, and yanked it down. There was a far-off *wooshing* sound, and a sickening drop. Far below in the endless acres of dirt and prairie grass, a small diner could be seen slumped like a beaten dog, with a flickering signpost reading, "Momma Chiffon's House Of Lard".

"I heard you're looking for musicians or something for tomorrow night." Lilith had come back in, and stood facing me as if nothing in the world should have my attention but herself.

"Not 'or something', but yes, we are looking for musicians," I said, trying not to make eye contact with her.

"Well, I dance. Beautifully. Mesmerizingly. I can dance while you play behind me–as my band."

"Thanks, but we aren't really looking for a dancer. Honestly, at this point, we are just trying to be as close as possible to what is expected of us so we'll get paid. I'm not really trying to make a bunch of big changes. This is just the easiest way I can think to get $500 for groceries for the crew."

She stood glaring, so I asked, "Do you sing?".

"I'm sure I can," she said.

And Tanner added, "I'm sure she's a great singer!"

"Well, we can try that, in moderation, if you really need to help." But I was beginning to realize this girl was going to be trouble.

A few minutes later, a small bird sitting on the roof of "Mamma Chiffon's House Of Lard" watched as the sky filled with a massive copper-colored Zeppelin, covered with patches, rust, dangling ropes, and emitting regular puffs of steam and smoke from various vents and chimneys.

From somewhere under the dangling ship-shaped cabin – a mismatched composite of what might have been trailer homes, submarines, part of a Victorian glass green-house, and what must have been the original naval construction – a hatch opened.

Out of it came a rope ladder on which hung Jean-Paul. Upon reaching the rooftop of the diner, he thrust a long greased hose down the kitchen chimney and started feeding it in yard by yard.

Down in the kitchen, Mamma Chiffon was barking orders at the new cook she'd hired the day before. "Girl, ain't nobody driving this highway gonna order a frilly thing like that. These people want chicken fried steak. They want waffles and mashed potatoes, they ain't gonna be ordering your highfalutin' pastries! I mean, what's this crust made outta, layers a' wax paper??"

"Filo," corrected the girl – tall, knobby-kneed and pig-tailed. It was Kristina. Behind her back, she stealthily grabbed the greasy hose, and guided it into the fry vats – all without Momma Chiffon noticing. Once the hose was in the grease, and as soon as Momma turned her massive behind toward her, Kristina gave three tugs on the hose, and quietly headed toward the back door.

The large slurping noise went unnoticed (as it was hardly out of place in this restaurant) and the vats began to empty.

Out in the gravel lot, Kristina swung one leg over my vintage motorcycle, and pulled a helmet out of the motorcycle's side-car. A large brown dog took the helmet's place. She revved the already running engine once, and sped off down the gravel highway.

Momma Chiffon heard this, rolled herself around and noticed the kitchen was empty. She also noticed the fry vats were empty, and a flicker of movement drew her eyes to the ceiling just as the hose slipped back into the chimney hole. None of this made enough sense to her to inspire an immediate reaction, and as she stood there trying to decide what flavor of mad to become (her default emotion), the sound of barking dogs and surprised rednecks started echoing from outside. She ran to the back door, and, hearing what sounded like massive outboard motors roaring from above her, she looked up in time to see a huge tail-fin slip out of view behind the roof's overhang.

Men were running from the diner to their rusted pick-ups, grabbing their requisite guns from their requisite rear window racks, while stubby pit bulls and Dobermans ran in circles barking at the sky.

A few shots were fired, as the huge oval silhouette slid over the parking lot and headed down the road. Trucks and bikers filled the lot with dust as they sped out after it.

Not too far down the road, Kristina and motorcycle screamed in angry acceleration, as Jean-Paul came up behind her on the still dangling rope ladder and attached a huge hook to the bike. Slowly, motorcycle, sidecar, girl, man, and the dog with ears flapping in the wind lifted from the dusty road and glided upward into the silent crimson night.

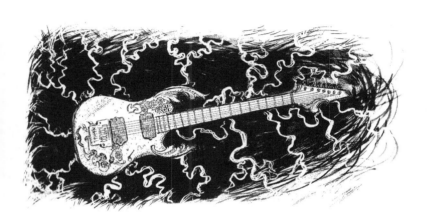

THE BEST GIMMICK EVER

The next night was the concert. Dr. Calgori had, in addition to overseeing the repairs and modifications to the *Ophelia*, spent some time repairing and upgrading our instruments. Our modern electric guitars, and synthesizers were, in his humble opinion, abysmally ugly. The doctor took it upon himself to correct this lack of design, and the result made our salvaged twentieth century instruments look like something from Captain Nemo's Nautilus.

That night as we packed up our instruments, Lilith came to us with a "new song" she had "written". But far from being a finished song and arrangement, this was merely the start of some sophomoric poetry. It was about a beautiful dancing girl, so beautiful the whole world loved her. I was supposed to finish this song for her, and then sing it while gazing at her as she danced before our audience.

"We do *not* have time to learn a new song! We've only got three hours until the show!" Kristina said coldly, as the rest of our make-shift ensemble continued to pack, avoiding eye contact with Lilith.

We arrived at the dingy roadside club at night. We doused all the lights onboard, and Daniel dropped down on a huge mooring hook, attaching the airship to an abandoned water tower a few dozen yards out of the reach of the light. After that, we lowered our gear and ourselves into the parking lot, just outside the ring of light created by the club. As long as we left before dawn, no one would know we hadn't just arrived in one of the many cars parked here.

The "festival" we were playing was called the Utah Dark Arts Festival. It was a once-a-year music event for Goths, and we were the third of four bands to play that night. Kristina, myself, Jean-Paul, Tanner, and Lilith entered in our strange Victorian attire, dragging our bizarrely modified equipment.

We told the stage manager we were the band Abney Park, and we were directed to the "dressing room", which in this case meant there were a bunch of mirrors propped up against beer kegs in the basement.

We stood out. The room was filled with tall shadowy musician-types; pale faced, in black eyeliner, black vinyl pants, turtle necks, mohawks, and massive black boots. In contrast we were comprised of: one kilted and top-hatted Tanner, Jean-Paul in his silk genie attire, myself in a tattered brown tailcoat I found in the previous captain's closet, Kristina wearing a borrowed (and too small) khaki military uniform, and Lilith looking like we stole her from a harem.

Musicians from other bands began to crowd around, gawking as we unpacked. I'd been afraid the clothes and instruments would draw attention in a bad way. Now I realized they were drawing attention in a good way.

As I unpacked my gear, the lead singer from the headline band called The Last Dance came up to me. "I absolutely love your new shtick! The band looks fantastic! I've never seen anything like this! Look at that guitar!" Jeff exclaimed, as Tanner pulled out a solid brass seven string guitar, complete with spinning clockwork, and firing sparks.

"Thanks!" interjected Lilith. "It was really my idea. I've been dressing them, and drawing pictures for them to copy…"

Kristina shot a glance as if to say, "Like hell you did," but a small crowd was now surrounding Lilith, and marveling at her genius.

"Of course, I didn't write the music. Honestly, the music sucks. Its not what I'm into at all," Lilith said casually, adjusting her small breasts in her corset in a very intentionally revealing way.

Still, I was just thrilled all these musicians liked it. I was afraid the result of our homemade gear and make-shift clothing would be laughter, or even worse. But people thought it was a new feature. "Um, yeah. We've got a new gimmick. You like it? And wait till you hear how our songs have...changed." This was a perfect cover. We have a new gimmick! Meanwhile, after the one rehearsal we fumbled through this morning, I was not confident we could sound anything like what was expected of us.

"I'm a bit curious *myself* as to how they will turn out." I mumbled this last bit to myself.

A huge, burly man with a tattooed neck and triple pierced nose appeared in the doorway. "Abney Park, five minutes," he growled at me.

We headed onstage, dragging our own gear. Copper guitar amplifiers, a two-hundred-year-old violin, rusty brass resonator mandolin, a bass guitar with copper tentacles coming out the sides, and synthesizer with tesla coils firing in the center.

The audience stood baffled and confused, and silent – but at least they hadn't left!

The first song began. It was an old guitar-driven piece I wrote years ago called "The Death of the Hero", but this time the guitar rhythm was replaced with violin, sounding more like a gypsy dance, than a rock song. Lilith spun and twirled, and writhed to it, and soon the audience was jumping in beat to the Sufi-style rhythm.

Then onto a bit I had written the day before: a song about an airship full of pirates, sneaking into town stealing parts for their ship. Again, instead of guitars, it lead in with a mandolin and puff organ duet between Kristina and Tanner. It was rapid fire, unexpected, and the audience was going wild! This new gimmick as they saw it was so fresh, so novel, and so thorough! "I almost *believe* it," they told themselves. "Its like I can hear a story running through the lyrics, song for song!" they said to their friends. We just smiled nervously, played our music, and hoped they didn't figure it out, which of course they never could. People have a hard time departing from what they know to be true, and this *couldn't* be true.

After the show, and several encores, the crew and the audience were buzzing with excitement over the concert. They loved the high energy of the music, the excitement of being in a strange place at a strange time, and the thrill of being onstage.

Again, Lilith stood in a crowd of fans taking credit for our changes, as the rest of us packed up our heavy equipment. The fact is, onstage she didn't do much more then swing her hips, but the fans enjoyed it so I had no complaints.

This was the crew's first exposure to the twenty-first century and modern music; and this was the twenty-first century's first exposure to our bizarrely anachronistic mix of sounds. Both were in love with each other.

VIRAL PIRACY

For a few days after the concert we remained aloft, trying to stay in a bank of clouds that was drifting slowly east, while Dr. Calgori calculated the return trip to 1906.

When he'd finished his calculations, the crew began to "batten down the hatches" as they put it, tying down anything that was precariously attached. Most of the crew had dread in their eyes. From what I heard, jumping through time wasn't easy. On the maiden voyage, the ship was so battered by the journey that she was nearly unrepairable. We had basically spent the last week repairing the damage from the first jump, and now we were about to do it again. The return jump would be equally as hard, although Calgori assured us he had braced the weaker parts of the structure. I consoled myself with the thought that they all knew what to expect now and should be better equipped to handle anything that might happen. The crew however, knowing what it would be like, fortified themselves with rum.

Finally, the hour came to make the jump. I stood at the massive captain's wheel, in what had become my quarters, having been warned that manning the "on deck bridge" was too dangerous. Daniel was at my side, holding onto two large brass handles that were attached to the ceiling. And Kristina and Tanner were sitting at the newly bolted down table and chairs to my right, throwing back shots of whiskey in order to prepare themselves for the turmoil of time travel. (I later learned this was the way of this crew: Daniel standing diligently ready to help, while the rest of the crew got drunk enough to overlook anything that needed doing!) Lilith was, confusingly, applying makeup with an air of complete confidence and lack of concern.

Finally, Calgori's voice could be heard through the 'yelly-phone', as I called it; a copper pipe that ran between the helm and the map room with a megaphone on each end. It really only worked if both parties yelled.

"With your permission, Captain, I'm ready to throw the switch."

I glanced at Tanner. He and Kristina threw back the contents of their shot glasses, before storing the glasses and bottle. I then looked back to Daniel, who pulled the rope of a steam whistle, notifying the rest of the crew we would soon be off.

"At your leisure, good Doctor!" I said, perhaps too enthusiastically.

At first there was no noise, but out of my peripheral vision, I could see the two glass orbs that hung outside my windows fill with pink glowing gas–a dark pink–the color of the sky during a lightning storm. Then came a shudder in the ship, followed by a slight and unnatural sense of anxiety. It was not like a panic attack, but like a feeling of acceleration that had nothing to do with moving or dropping. My ears popped painfully.

Instantly, a huge wind hit the ship, as if a wall of stone was thrown against us! Windows smashed, lanterns swung and shattered against the wall, a rack of decorative swords and rifles crashed to the ground and flew across the floor.

Daniel swung nearly perpendicular on his handles, and hung there as the ship lurched to one side.

There was a massive groaning of ropes from outside the cabin, and the huge "*pling!*" of at least one rope snapping loose. From elsewhere in the ship I could hear men yelling back and forth to each other.

Rain was now pelting the glass. Doctor Calgori later told me the rain was from a change in air pressure between the time we left and the time we arrived and the varying altitudes we could be at. As the two different air pressures collided, a small but dramatic weather system would form. Occasionally, this would even cause snow.

Finally, slowly, almost as if in slow motion, a bookshelf toppled from the wall, and crashed to the floor, spilling books everywhere.

This was too much for Kristina and Tanner, and they burst into drunken laughter.

Within a few minutes, the swinging and shaking slowed to a gentle back and forth rocking, like a ship on mild waves. Daniel relaxed his grip on his handles, let his feet back to the floor, and sarcastically said, "Well, that was fun! Let's get on deck and see *when* we are, because at this point I *totally* trust the Doctor to stick to the plan!"

As we left the cabin, Tanner was already pouring Kristina and himself another round.

Daniel and I emerged at the same time most of the rest of the crew was coming on deck. The clouds around us were burning off as fast as ice melts on a stove top, and they soon gave way to a warm and beautiful day. There were blue skies around us, and emerald green seas below. In the very far distance to our rear we could see a coast lined with palm trees.

Below and just ahead of us, sailing away from the coast was a large three-masted ship low in the water and heavily laden with cargo. It had four cannon ports per side, and the deck was crowded with black-skinned, nearly naked African tribal people, sitting so tightly packed it seemed at first as though we were looking at a shipload of carved statues.

Daniel and I extended our spyglasses. A closer look showed that the dark-skinned people were captives, chained to each other, and chained to the boat itself.

Then we saw a horrendous sight! At the aft of the ship, four clothed and fair-skinned men were struggling with one of the captives. His back was criss-crossed with blood: he had obviously been whipped, and the blood was running down his legs and arms, making it hard for the fair-skinned men to hold him. They each had an arm or a leg, and as we watched, they tossed the body of the struggling man right off the ship!

A mother held her screaming toddlers tightly to her naked breast, turning their faces away. One small boy of perhaps eight ran to the men screaming in rage, and was stopped by the sole of a boot that shattered his nose and covered his face in blood. This was obviously the ejected man's wife and childern. It was her turn to be a strong mother and quiet her childern: so she grabbed the eight-year-old, and held him down with the others. Toddlers didn't become useful for many years, so they had no value. Later, when they slept, this young mother, now a young widow, would allow herself to cry–but not now. What was left of her family relied on her keeping control.

I dropped my glass from my now red and moist eyes, and turned to Daniel.

"Where the hell are we?" I choked out. "What the hell is this?"

"I think that's a slave ship. That coast must be Africa, and this is a ship headed for the Carribean."

Doctor Calgori hobbled in between us "Then I'm afraid I have made some minor mistake in my calculations. This is the location I was targeting, but I did not intend to travel this far back in time. The slave trade was outlawed in 1806. If that's a slave ship, we are one hundred years past our target, or say, one hundred years too early."

I turned to Daniel and said, "Daniel, get to the lower crow's nest...and loose the rope ladder!" Being a soldier, he was immediately in motion, but he yelled back over his shoulder as he climbed over the side rail, "Robert, what are we doing???"

"We are saving a father, then a family, and then we are going to hurt some bad guys!" I replied.

In retrospect, this was a rash move. There are times to think, and times to move. This wasn't the time to think – this father would be dead soon. Perhaps my rash actions were the result of dormant and, as of yet, unneeded heroic tendencies. Or perhaps they were the result of the rum in my belly, put there to calm my nerves. Perhaps the rest of the crew were so easily swayed to this new task because they themselves had been drinking.

Or perhaps we are *all* born to be hereos.

I sprinted to the bow-helm, and pushed on the elevator wheel, which lurched the huge airship into a steep dive. "Easy, Captain, nearly lost Daniel there!" yelled Jean-Paul as he watched over the railing.

From where I stood, I couldn't see the underside crow's nest, but I could see the surface of the ocean approaching rapidly. "Jean-Paul, tell me when the lower mast is a few feet from the water, then get down there and help Daniel."

Jean-Paul watched for a few seconds, then yelled "THREE... TWO...ONE...LEVEL OFF!".

I heaved the elevator wheel, and the ship slowly began to arch towards a level positon, but much too slowly! There was a hard jerk, followed by a spray of foam at the back of the ship, as the mast dipped in. Water was tossed twenty feet high behind us, and a huge *crack*! sounded from deep in the hull as the mast splintered.

The African that had been tossed overboard was vainly swimming toward the ship that had dropped him. I saw him quickly dissappear from my view under our bow. I just had time to think *"Shit, that was quick! I hope Daniel and Jean-Paul had time to…"*

"HUZZAH! They got him!" yelled the crew watching from our side. I pushed a little harder and our airship began to climb again, then I handed the wheel to one of the other pilots and ran to the edge.

As he climbed over the airship's railing, I could see the African was tall, even taller than me, and rippling with blue-black muscles like a race horse who had just finished his race. He had tattooing, or a sort of decorative scarring on his face and shoulders, and his eyes burned with fear and anger as his arms shook with adrenaline from the cold of the sea water in the wind of our forward movement.

He stood dripping on the deck in a circle of our crew. Not knowing who this new group of strangely dressed men were, there was a brief moment when it looked like he would spring on us. Since nobody could translate our intentions to him, I spoke to him in a language a father could understand: I put my sword in his hand, and pointed toward his family's captors.

Then I turned and yelled to the crew, "Full speed ahead! Daniel, you've got about forty-five seconds to assemble twenty of your toughest fighters! Each man should carry three swords, and at least two men will need bolt cutters or very large hammers."

"I think I understand you. I'm on it!" Daniel yelled, and the entire crew was in motion.

I ran back to the stern-helm and noticed that although this slave ship was the first ship, this was not the only ship in the water. Five hundred yards to port was a gunship, an escort to the other. It was altering its course now to converge on us. *"Shit,"* I thought, *"this is not going to be easy."*

Daniel and twenty burly armed sailors were starting to climb over the side, and down the ladders to the lower crow's nest. One of them was Tanner. I grabbed him by the shoulder, "There's a lot of whiskey in you my friend, can you do this?"

"If there wasn't, I couldn't! In my present condition, however, I'm more than enthusiastic to do this!" he replied with a starry-eyed grin.

"Good point. Hand me your bottle." I pulled the cork with my teeth, and threw back almost more than I could take without it coming back on me. As it burned in my throat, I vaulted over the railing. *God, I hate whiskey.*

We were converging on the slave ship at a startling pace. Our sails were still down, but our propellers were roaring, and before I had a chance to wonder if I could make it to the bottom before we collided, I saw the mast of the slave ship tangle with our own lower mast. Simultaneously, the rear of the slave ship lifted from the water, while the bow of the *Ophelia* pitched forward, and several of our sailors were knocked from the rigging to the slave-filled decks below.

The slavers were ready, having watched our odd vehicle grab their discarded slave. They had a few minutes while we approached to get over the shock of a flying ship, and they leaped on our men the second we fell amongst the Africans. But here they got a surprise!

Bear with me while I explain. If the singer of a rock band leaps from a stage into a massive and excited crowd, the crowds put their hands upward and "crowd surfs" him. They hold him aloft and move him around the room as if he was surfing on his back. In fact this is called "crowd surfing". Likewise, when the slavers leaped into the crowd of chained slaves to attack us, the slaves were not idle. They also had seen us pick up one of their own, and they saw us attacking their captors. So when the slavers entered the crowd of slaves, a hundred hands picked them up and tossed them overboard!

In under a minute, only eighteen slave ship sailors remained, and they crowded into the center of the deck, back-to-back, keeping as far from the Africans as possible. Soon much of the crew of the *Ophelia* stood on deck too, some starting to cut loose and arm the grateful captives. We cut the slaves' chains with large bolt cutters we had taken from the hardware store in Idaho in 2006.

The last man to climb down onto this ship was the African we pulled from the water. With no hesitation whatsoever he strode to the captain of the slave ship, raised skyward the heavy cutlass I gave him, and cleaved the captain's face and chest with one blow.

He then turned and knelt, and embraced his newly freed children as the rest of my crew ran past him and threw themselves into battle.

This was to me my first *real* sword fight, but before you doubt the likelihood of my survial, let me say that I was on the fencing team both in high school, and college, and I had half a bottle of cheap whiskey in me to keep my mind from telling me that these were actually sharpened blades!

We, and the now free and armed slaves, took no time whatsoever to mince their captors. As the fighting began to slow, I noticed my left arm was bleeding quite a lot, and as I looked at it I heard a series of deep booms from our starboard side, followed by a shower of wood chips coming from above us!

The escort ship, which I had forgotten until now, had come within range and observed the whole fight. They were now firing on the *Ophelia*! The first volley had smashed the wood of her belly, and pieces of that wood were raining down on our heads. The ship was a war ship, huge and strong, and its crew were not slavers, but naval warriors. I could only watch as they fired a second round into our beautiful airship!

As I stood there, useless, wondering what I could do from here, wondering how many hits our airship could take, I heard a distant, cockneyed voice above me yell, "Return Volley!" and suddenly the starboard side of the *Ophelia* erupted in flame and smoke, from OUR cannons!

Daniel laid a hand on my shoulder. "Have no fear, Robert. The *Ophelia* is an airborne war ship, more than a hundred years newer in design than that ship in the water. She was built to overturn battles. This will not be difficult."

Our first volley cracked railings and decking on the escort ship, and either by good luck, skill, or fierce and vengeful Karma, one cannon ball went directly through the attacking ship's captain!

As our crew loaded for the second round, I hoisted myself into the rigging, and yelled, "Surrender now, and be set free. Otherwise, prepare to die! I've got fifty cannon (I was not sure if this was true) and a hundred sailors (I'm certain this was not true) and we can sink you from a height your guns cannot reach, if we choose! LAY DOWN YOUR ARMS!"

Instantly the lower-ranked sailors began to drop their swords or step back from the cannons. The officers frantically conversed before one yelled back to me, "Hold your fire! What are your terms?" There was obvious panic in his voice.

"Surrender with no more protest, and we'll set you adrift in your dinghies. From here you should be able to return to the shore, but your ship we take! This ship is too crowded. I've got a boat load of Maasai here that I think look like they could use it."

In the months that followed, the seas became thick with tribal African warriors. We taught them to sail, and use cannon, and together we sought other slave ships and their escorts. Two ships quickly became four, and four became eight and then twenty, and so on. Each slave ship they overtook added sailors and warriors to their crews, and each escort ship they defeated added to the size of their armada.

In under a year, the slave trade was eradicated between Africa and the Americas. Soon the nations of the world had to ask permission from the United Tribal Navy of Africa for permission to sail through their waters. UTNA was swift, and strong, and merciless.

The night of our rescue, as I sat in the captain's cabin, undressing for bed, I noticed in the corner of the room a device that looked like an antique typewriter with a small TV screen attached to the top. A plaque on the bottom read: "Chronofax, by Calgori Industries". *Now how did that get here*, I wondered.

I went over to it and typed,

Dear little boy.

It looks like you were right, so I dropped that
worthless life. Things are really looking up for
us. Wait till I tell you what you will become when
you grow up! Rock star. Airship Captain. Pirate!
Oh, and you'll also be a hero. Better practice
your swordsmanship.

As I typed this message to myself, I could swear I remembered receiving it…was I typing this from memory, or making it up?

I pulled out my journal, and sketched these lyrics:

Letters Between a Little Boy
and Himself As An Adult

Dear Mr. Brown,
One day I'll be you and
Although I'm only eight now,
You need to hear my rules.
Never stop playing
Never stop dreaming and
And be careful not to
Turn into someone we'd hate.

Dear little boy,
I'm doing my best up here but
It's a thankless job and
Nobody feels the same.
You work long hours,

Watch your credit rating,
Pay your taxes and
Prepare to die.

Hey, Mr. Brown,
That can't be what life is like!
I've watched some movies,
And I've read some books.
Life should be exciting
And sometimes scary but
What you're describing doesn't
Seem worth the time.

Hey little boy,
I think you were always right
I've dropped that worthless life and
I'm moving on.
Life should be adventure,
I'm stealing back my soul,
I've lost too many years now
I'm awake.

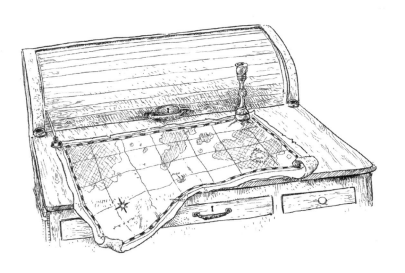

NEW PLANS

"Seriously, what the hell was that?" said Daniel as he strode into the map room. Most of the crew, Dr. Calgori, and myself had assembled to talk about our rescue from the previous day.

"That was bloody brilliant, is what it was!" replied the salty giant, Mongrel, once again mopping under his eye patch with a dirty rag, but grinning from ear to ear. "It was like a good round o' piracy, but instead of stealing from people, we was stealing *people* back for dem'selves!" Then he pause, with a concerned look. "Not that I'd know what piracy was like. I was just imagining what it *must* be like, I guess." And he nervously looked at his feet.

"It was drunken, emotional rashness," said the Doctor. "But I also agree with Mongrel, it was brilliant. It would appear the man we borrowed from the future has leadership skills, as well as piloting skills. I set him to learn to pilot the *Ophelia* and nothing more. Yet before you know it, he's barking orders and you're all following them, much to the benefit of mankind!"

"You're overstating what happened," said Daniel dryly. "The crew was following orders from him, because the last captain was also our pilot."

"We'll see," said Calgori. "In the meantime, I think he should take over captain's duties. We don't currently have a captain, and the crew seems eager to follow him. Plus, he carries a broader knowledge of history than any of us. We need someone in charge with a bird's-eye view of what will happen over the next few hundred years."

Daniel opened his mouth again to object, but Calgori interrupted him "No, this wouldn't be following standard procedure. But I dare say we are not, in fact, following any laws but our own at the moment. If you press a ship full of pirates and criminals, you'll end up with a ship run by pirates and criminals!

Who among us would care to return to Victorian England at this point and offer up our ship's log, outlining our theft, and drunken attacks on what would have otherwise been a profitable enterprise for the English crown?"

No one had a response.

"At this point, I think we are now on our own agenda. Robert, will you do us the honor of captaining this vessel?" Calgori asked.

"I will!" I said, and the crew cheered! Well, some of them made enthusiastic noises, if I remember correctly. Daniel certainly did not.

"So then, what do we do now? Are we to be employed with escorting the Maasai on the quest to overthrow slave ships?" Tanner said.

"We could. But no, I think we have a greater duty." Doctor Calgori replied, "Throughout time, there have been incredible injustices to mankind, by mankind. Right up until our glorious age, mankind never stopped inflicting terrors on itself. And unless I'm greatly mistaken, our new Captain, Robert, can probably tell us of a few that happened after our time." Here he paused for me to speak.

"It's true," I said " Every decade seems to have its world wars, and some of them have eclipsed anything you have ever seen. We've had government planned nation-wide starvation, and genocide…and that's just off the top of my head."

"I feel we have a machine now that, for the first time since the dawn of man, can actually UNDO the things mankind has done wrong," the doctor continued. "It won't be easy, rulers do not easily change their mind by persuasion, so I'm afraid we'll have to stop them by force."

Daniel interrupted, "But a captain should have…"

He was interrupted in turn by Dr. Calgori dramatically collapsing into his cane and saying, "This would be easier if I hadn't gotten so damned old! I feel so tired now. Kristina, can you help me to my cabin? Robert, speak with Daniel. Think up our next move! Let's right the wrongs of history…together!" He trailed off in a coughing fit, as Kristina helped him out of the room.

Daniel protested, but less now than before, and it was not long before he was starting to get excited about this new mission. The more we made plans, the more excited he got. He was a proper military man, but he was also an *American* army officer, who I am guessing was imprisoned after being caught on a covert mission. He seemed glad to no longer be pressed into service for another country. We didn't stop our enthusiastic planning until just before sunrise.

Kristina told me later that as she helped the Doctor into bed, she asked him why he had so surprisingly pushed for me as the captain.

"When I first created this vessel," he said, "it was for *science*. I didn't care how that science was applied after I had finished, I just wanted to achieve it, and I couldn't achieve it without military funding. But the more I heard of how they planned to use this vessel, the more I realized I had to get it out of their hands, or at least change the plan. Daniel was likely to be next-in-line to command it, and he's a good man, but his nature is to follow the orders and objectives laid out to him at the start of a mission by a superior."

And then he took a more apologetic tone. "But with Robert as Captain there seems little chance that this vessel will continue on its original mission. He was not a pirate, so I didn't see him using it for personal gain. My impression was that he was motivated more for the sake of earning the title of 'hero' than anything else. That seemed the least dangerous motivator for a new captain."

"I'm surprised by how well you seem to know Robert, after such a short time." Kristina then asked while helping the doctor into his bunk, "But are you saying you did something to the old captain?"

"Of course I did!" he answered with mock pride. "Well, I put things into motion that ended him. People are easy to motivate, and motivating pirates towards revenge is particularly easy."

The doctor laid his gray fragile head on the rough pillow, "And I feel no guilt. If he hadn't made so many enemies in the short time he'd been captain, he wouldn't have been so easy to dispatch." He closed his eyes, and mumbled, "Imagine the damage he would have done if the world's most powerful weapon had been left in his hands."

THE BATTLE OF ARCOT

To hear history books tell the story, the Battle of Arcot was a heroic example of an underdog, Robert Clive, fighting against insurmountable odds. By "using his clever wit", he "overcomes insurmountable odds and saves the day". In truth, the odds were grossly in his favor. Robert Clive took the city of Arcot with more than five thousand soldiers, easily defeating a part-time militia. He seized food, supplies, wells, and enslaved the city in the name of the East India Company. By holding the city of Arcot, the British Crown divided the forces of Chanda Sahib, which would weaken India's defenses against this conquering nation. Ultimately, this would bring about the fall of India as an independent nation for the next one hundred years to come.

Even if you overlook the military advantage of holding the city of Arcot, you still have a city being held by an evil empire. I'm not passing judgment on England; to the best of my knowledge most countries have been "Evil Empires" at some time or another. This was their era. I lived in India as a small boy while my mother did anthropological fieldwork there, so when conversation in the map room turned to "what shall we do next" it occurred to me that if we overturned that one battle, we could overturn decades of the slavery of India.

As we appeared over the city in 1751, Clive's fortifications of the city easily held out against the surrounding forces of Chanda Sahib.

From above, the city looked like the geometric pattern of a Persian carpet. A patchwork of walls and buildings with circular towers placed at each corner, British cannons bristled from the tower sides like points of stars. There were square courtyards, with little flower-shaped wells or fountains in the middle, and little patchwork-like buildings, crawling with people. Lines of regimented soldiers could be seen placed around crowds of the native city dwellers.

We were still very high up, and we could see tents to the southwest, and barracks, and the war beasts of Chanda's forces. Not a small force, but it was ill-equipped to withstand the British cannons Clive had placed in the many towers around the city. Even if Chanda could have reached the walls without the cannons pummeling his soldiers into the bloody sand, all he could have done was stand at the gate of the city and knock.

The hot wind of summer dusk was blowing little spirals of dust below us as we slipped over the walls of the city toward the siege camps. Boys, tiny in the distance below us, ran along the city walls yelling up at us. Some met the butt of a rifle from Clive's border guards.

We descended our rope ladders at gunpoint in the middle of an empty elephant paddock. Ironically, one of our Victorian sailors had learned to speak Hindi when he was stationed in the still occupied India one hundred years in the future. He had a tough time convincing turbaned soldiers that we shared a common enemy, and were here to help. It was obvious that we *could* help–our flying warship was holding Chanda's soldiers in awe. Our skin color and accents were no different from the enemy's (with a few exceptions among the crew) but I think in the end it was our clothes that convinced them we had nothing to do with the East India Company.

That night we met with Chanda and his generals. We told them we were sent from a country called "Imairika", and that the English were our common foe. Hell, it might have been true at that time. We made plans that night, and preparations for two days, and during this time the camp was filled with hustling craftsmen.

As the morning sun of the third dawn stained the city a peach-gold color, Robert Clive's soldiers saw a puzzling sight.

Over the city walls appeared the sails of a ship, surrounding a massive canvas balloon. As the hull of our ship appeared, the soldiers sounded alarms, and ran with rifles to the walls.

On the city towers, cannons fired their shots, but our height was greater than they were used to firing on and they narrowly missed our airship. Their shots fell back into the city amongst the troops now swarming the walls. *Ophelia's* cannons erupted in an angry retort – dozens of shots causing the soldiers in the southern tower to leap into the moat, while the *Ophelia's* cannon turned the northeast tower to dust.

Now the *Ophelia* was high above the southwest wall of the city, and under it hung a huge platform, nearly as big as *Ophelia's* hull. Her bow dipped as the ship and platform slipped down toward the city's main open square.

A company of one hundred British soldiers marched into the square. They were regimented, and well-groomed in their blue-gray uniforms–freshly laundered by the women of Arcot–and tall black boots–polished nightly by orphaned children of the city. They acted unimpressed by our flying ship, and raised their rifles toward the platform we carried, awaiting the Indian soldiers they expected to run out. But more than one eyebrow was raised at what they actually saw.

As the massive timbers of the platform kicked the courtyard's dust in the air, up stood a half-dozen armored elephants. On their brass-plated backs were turbaned soldiers armed with pachyderm-mounted swivel cannons (borrowed from *Ophelia*), and even a couple full-sized cannons. The massive beasts thundered forward into the British soldiers, scattering their ranks as the swivel guns pounded and crumbled the perches of the snipers on the walls around them.

After the elephants left the platform, a dozen ropes dropped from the belly of *Ophelia*, and down slid our pirates and myself; pistols tucked in belts, swords strapped to our backs. At this point, our crew had had many months of fighting together, and this kind of attack was old hat to us.

As soon as the courtyard defenses were dispersed, we turned the largest elephants toward the gates. These massive gates stood under a huge stone bridge, and faced the outside world with six-inch thick iron plates. But from the inside, our target was simply one large wooden beam that horizontally braced the doors, two feet by three feet thick.

Three or four British soldiers were stationed behind the doors, and each dared no more then a single hurried shot toward the charging, armored elephants before fleeing to small side-passageways.

To protect the elephants' ears from the sound of the cannon, each had been packed that morning with clay and cloth. This kept the beasts from rearing up as the massive ten pounders shot through the wooden beam, splinters and smoke filled the air as they ran on. The ear-packs also kept the beasts from hearing their master's commands to "Thehar Jaana!" and the gates smashed open as the stunned elephants tripped on the wooden splinters and rolled, crushing their riders and armor.

Clive's soldiers stood on the dusty bricks in the doorway, rifles at their shoulders. As the first of the Indians rushed in the doors, British guns went off. Bullets found their mark in the massive shoulders of Chandra's front guard but that hardly slowed their pace. Their objective was to push back the British guard enough to allow the rest of the army to enter the city.

I saw this from the center of the square, and gestured to the remaining elephants' riders to come in behind the British troops. The ground then erupted in front of me, and a group of five gray coated infantry men ran in firing at me.

I leaped toward a small arched tunnel in the wall, and ran into the dark wet interior. I didn't look back, but in a few minutes I heard them enter the tunnel behind me. There were no turns, only doors that I could not risk the time to check and see if they were locked, but ahead of me I could see green-golden daylight.

Soon I burst into the light, and it was as if I'd entered a new world. The sound of gunfire was distant and muted. My feet slipped on hard packed red mud, and all around me was lush thick vegetation: vines, leaves the size of dinner plates, and tree trunks the size of small houses.

There were more rifles firing behind me, *these guys are determined!* They must have noticed I was giving orders, and figured I was worth the pursuit.

I stumbled forward. The mud clung to my boots as I ran, and with each step my feet got heavier with the weight of it. Eventually I found myself running on ancient carved stones. I was running out of breath. Cardio is hard to achieve on a flying boat with few large rooms! Ahead of me I saw some nearly fallen arches and the red stone domes of an old shrine.

I ran into the intricately carved building and around a corner to catch my breath. Vines and branches had been tearing the place apart slowly over hundreds of years. My eyes darted quickly around for a hiding place or a way out. I noticed in an alcove behind me that the large, silent and hooded head of a cobra was rising angrily out of a crushed pot he'd been sleeping in. At this point the first of the British soldiers plunged into the hall. The cobra struck at me, and having been staring right at him, I tried to jump back and tripped.

It's a good thing I did; something about the angle my leg

caught on the fallen bricks threw me to the ground much faster then I could have on my own. The cobra, missing me, leapt right on the soldier. The soldier let out a scream (*was that the Wilhelm Scream??*) and the startled snake bit him. The soldier brushed the snake frantically from him and ran out of the tunnel with an "Oooh! Ooh! OOH!" Poor guy, he'd surely die of that bite a lot slower than he would have with a bullet.

At this point I noticed a hole in the ceiling above the alcove, and I clamored up. Once on top of the temple I found myself in a knot of branches and leaves, and I crept through them across the rooftops back in the direction I thought the city must be.

An hour later, I found myself back inside the city walls, and discovered the battle pretty much over. Daniel had what remained of Robert Clive's forces on their knees at gun point. Their rifles had been placed on a cart that was being wheeled out the front gate. Clive himself stood in his luxurious, but bloodied, uniform looking disgusted at us all.

"How DARE you! Some of you even look English! Explain yourselves before I have you in irons!" he said. I got to hand it to him, he had balls.

"I'll explain," I said. "You think your power has given you immunity. You followed orders expertly enough to allow yourself to be god of this city. It all worked, as long as you didn't think about the monstrous things you were ordered to do. Since the order came from above, you figured no one could hold you responsible." I leaned in close. "Well, think again."

The city of Arcot was returned to the people of India. With this new foothold, Chandra's forces gained size and strength. As the rumor of our attack on Robert Clive's forces spread across India, it seemed to have the effect of uniting the people of India in a way they hadn't been before, and their pride strengthened them. Never again would another force take control of their country. Well, not for a couple hundred years, anyway.

Everybody was thrilled with the outcome. Everybody except Lilith, that is. She stomped about for days, grumbling to any of our crew that would listen to her about how she wasn't "allowed" to do anything in the battle, grumbling how much better it would have gone had she played a larger part.

She grumbled to me about it once, to which I responded, "You determine your own level of involvement. If you have something to contribute, please do. It's not my job to invent a way for you to be useful." I suppose I might have said too much but, dammit, I want to enjoy success, not listen to someone bitch that our success wasn't attributed enough to them. She, of course, stormed out, slamming the door behind her.

We stayed in the city for a couple weeks, resting and repairing, and healing. One night, very late, and after a huge celebration with way too much drinking, Kristina came into our little apartment in the city looking tired, but angry. "Something's going down wrong," she said, pointing at the door. "The crew seems mad as hell. They are saying some very bad things. You need to get out there! It sounds like mutiny!"

"What the hell!?!? What could anyone be mad about!?! All we've been doing is laying around accepting praise and food for weeks!" I was drunk, and half asleep, but I felt my face getting red with anger. Emotions come prematurely when you've been drinking.

I threw a shirt over my shoulders, and stumbled out of the apartment while still pulling on my boots. My face was warm with drink, and my mind was foggy.

I found a group of most of the higher-ranking crew sitting around a couple tables in the main square. Everyone but Doctor Calgori, who would have gone to bed hours ago. It was pitch black, around 3 a.m., and by the multi-colored lantern light, I could see the tables were strewn with empty bottles. I pulled up a chair at the end of one table. Tanner sat at it, with Daniel, Mongrel, Jean-Paul, and Lilith. All but Lilith had dark looks on their faces. She wore a look of calm, defiant victory.

"So, what are we talking about?" I asked. I meant to say it calm and collectedly, but thanks to the rum I'm fairly sure I blurted it out angrily and defensively.

"Don't play stupid, Cap'n!" Mongrel growled. "We're on to ya." Everyone scowled with red eyes. Lilith spun a finger in her drink carelessly, and licked it.

"Seriously, Daniel, what's going on?" I asked. Daniel was the professional here, I could ask him.

"Here is the thing," Daniel began in his official 'calm things down' voice. "The crew knows what you're planning. And they don't like it. We need you to know one thing: if you go through with it, the next time we are in battle together, we are not going to fight with you."

"WHAT!?!" I was baffled. "Then we'll all die! My god, what do you think I'm planning?"

"You are planning to get rid of Lilith." Tanner said, face red with anger, fists clenched.

"What? Why would I do that?" I asked. Now Lilith was making eye contact. She was daring me to deny it. I took a breath, and started slowly. "Honestly, no, I wasn't going to 'get rid of anyone'. Why would I want to? Everything is going perfectly. We've had success at everything we've done!"

"You've always hated me! You won't let me do anything, onstage or during missions!" she blurted out. "You've been planning to leave me here in the city, or sell me into slavery! You know I would be a better captain than you, so you keep me hidden." She lashed out at me, her tone dripping with poison and self-pity.

"What the hell? No! I haven't been planning any such thing! Honestly, I don't really think about you that much!"

"That was cruel, Robert!" Tanner declared blackly. "Why won't you let her do anything during missions?"

"Look, I just assign people jobs based on their skills and what needs to be done. If we don't need a belly dancer during a mission, I don't have a lot for her to do." I paused. "She gets most of the attention when we play concerts! Lilith, people love you, and you don't even do that much! You should be happy about that!" I was trying to console and calm her, though frankly, now I was thinking that getting rid of her was a good idea.

"Look, you guys are threatening mutiny over something you *think* I might *eventually* do. I had no such idea in my head. But mutiny during a battle will kill us all!" I paused again. "There is way too much drink at this table, and in us. None of us is handling this well. You have to know I have no plans of getting rid of anyone!" I finished.

"Well, if you do…" Tanner threatened, "Don't expect us to stand by you."

I stood up, a look of apprehension and puzzlement on my face. The pretty little girl was unhappy with her lot, and was attempting to change her lot by throwing a tantrum. A mutiny would be caused by any actions the crew perceived as me doing anything wrong to her. Part of this was true, I didn't have a huge use for her, but that didn't mean I was attempting to get rid of her either. She was fine as she was, but now, she was a time bomb waiting to go off. The trigger would be me trying to get rid of her, so all I could do was wait for it to explode.

I spent the night by myself on one of the castle walls. This should have been a victory, but somehow I had emerged a villain. I watched the sun rise, contemplating my options. I wasn't sure I had any.

I pulled out my journal, and sketched some lyrics in it:

My Life

My love, my life, my band, my wife.

I got lost. I get used. Take the praise, and abuse.

Am I the hero in my own day dream?

Or am I the villain, are things as they seem?

Am I the villain in my own daydream?

Am I the hero, are things as they seem?

WHAT THE HELL WAS THAT?

After Arcot, we refueled, and re-crewed. The *Ophelia* didn't actually lose many lives, but in the weeks that followed we were so pampered in the city of Arcot that many chose to stay. The city, once cleaned up, was beautiful, and we spent a lot of time on deep carpets, eating curry fed to us by beautiful girls in colorful silk saris. I'll be honest, it was hard to leave, and not everybody was willing to go. We lost more men to the beautiful young women of India than we lost to Robert Clive's soldiers.

I found the crew also spent a lot of time selling things they'd stolen in 2006. Flashlights, iPods, sneakers, you name it. Despite the fact that these goods were not paid for in my time, I suppose this is an honest trade route. Trading through time; buying products where they are common, and selling where they are scarce is the essence of "trade". And this trade became a big part of how we paid for things we weren't given. Selling antiques, or future-artifacts to another time became part of our business. Still, a little voice quietly whispered in my head, *don't let Calgori find out.*

After a month we finally departed, and by this time some of our crew had been replaced with brave young lads from the city. Next to the sunburned and scarred pirates we now had brown skin, turbans,and punjabi-pants, and we had curved scimitars next to the long straight British blades. They all joined us on our quest through time to right the wrongs of Mankind.

We continued month-after-month, looking through history books we had taken to find injustices of the past. We'd then travel back to a time when we were technologically superior to our opponents, and we'd snuff out the injustices we saw there. Time after time we would eliminate misdeeds, and time after time would we wipe the tarnish from history. Preventing scabs by stopping the wound from occurring.

People from those times and cultures would join us and add to our crew, which in turn added to our knowledge of history and to our ability to overturn wrongs we saw in the past.

We had become some sort of super-chronological heroes; at least in our own eyes. We had more success than failure, but there were plenty of embarrassing moments. The longer we "helped" the more often we'd encounter people who didn't want our help.

Also, I was beginning to see that heroics requires a forced naivety. I'll explain:

Imagine a hypothetical valley with one river and two parched cities who need the water. If one city diverted the river to save its people and crops, the other city would go without water. This deprived city would in turn fight to survive. War.

"Why not share the water?" you might ask. Well, in this hypothetical struggle, imagine there was only enough water for one city's people and crops. Who, then, is the villain, and who is the damsel to be saved? It became harder and harder to find an obvious "right side" to defend, and we learned that most often both sides were right.

It felt like heroes weren't wanted, or welcome. And sometimes it felt like we'd force ourselves to choose one party's perspective, just for the rush of ending the week feeling like heroes again. *Try not to think about that other city.*

As far as the crew went, things were tense. Deep inside I now carried the bitterness of their threatened mutiny, and a fear I would do or say something wrong that would bring it out again. I made the crew "vote" on everything, and I wouldn't even voice my opinions, for fear of what would happen if they disagreed with my vote.

I was still called "Captain" but often I wondered if it was said ironically. It seemed the term "captain" now meant, "someone to handle all the uncomfortable decisions nobody else wanted to think about, and someone to take the blame when things went wrong." I certainly didn't feel I was in charge anymore, or got credit for our successes. I seemed only responsible for negative outcomes. If I gave an order it was followed…but only if they were going to do it anyway. If they didn't feel like doing it, they would give me a weak excuse of why they didn't like the idea, and walk away.

I was captain, it was *supposed* to be my choice, but it stopped feeling like I even had a say.

Things with Lilith started to get a bit better. I think she was enjoying her victory. I tried to pay more attention to her, since it was that, or wait for her to stage another possible mutiny. The result was she calmed down a bit. She befriended Kristina, and hung out with the two of us often. *Yeah, fun, right?*

This was not enjoyable for me. It's not that she wasn't clever, or witty, or fun to be around. It's just that I felt like I was walking on eggshells filled with gunpowder: step too hard, and we all would die.

One evening, as I was piloting the late shift through a bank of thoroughly drenching clouds (toward a city we were told would have replacement canvas for our sails and gas bag), Kristina, Lilith and I stood on deck. Lilith had drawn some sketches of some ideas she had. Plans she was making for our next mission, things she thought would make the airship more stable. Plans that really didn't sound like they were going to work, but I nodded and smiled and said, "Sure, we can talk about this with the rest of the officers, and see what everybody thinks. Let's see if Calgori likes that idea, that's sort of his call, but I think it looks great! Nice work!" I tried to make it sound as if I liked the ideas, without committing to any of them. I tried to always agree, while neither committing nor condescending. I didn't want to crack the egg and lose a foot.

Finally, Kristina got tired. She'd stopped responding to the endless soliloquy of self-aggrandizing, yet worthless, ideas pouring out of Lilith. All at once, in the middle of one of Lilith's sentences, Kristina blurted, "I'm tired, I'm going to bed", and she tromped below deck.

This was uncomfortable. I was now on my own, to walk over the explosive eggshells by myself. I couldn't excuse myself since someone had to steer the boat.

She went on explaining her ideas, verbally patting herself on the back for things either the rest of the crew had already thought of and dismissed, or would never agree to attempt. While talking, she leaned in close to show me her sketches under the lamplight.

I zoned out. I started to become acutely aware of everything but what she was saying. I could hear the soaking wet lanyards creaking as the ship slowly rocked back and forth, swinging from the airbag on which it hung. I could feel the canvas of my pants sticking wetly to my thighs, the sleeves of my coat sticking to my arms. I could hear the mild hissing and popping of the propane lantern above me, as it struggled to push light through the fog. And I could feel Lilith's chest press against mine… And then it happened. *She kissed me!* She kissed me, right on the goddamn mouth! Just when I was slipping into a beautiful zen moment of ignoring the crap out of her, she slipped up into the space between my arms and the captains wheel, and that size 2 Judas kissed me!

I let go of the wheel and took a couple steps backwards,

"What the hell was that?" I blurted out. "Are you trying to get me into trouble?"

"No", she said, skillfully pouty.

"Then what the hell was that?"

"Well," she paused, probably noticing the horrified look of a trapped animal that was carved into my brow. "I made a pact with myself. I decided I would have no more regrets in life." She said it in the same polished and self-aware tones she always used, as if she had rehearsed all her lines weeks before performing them.

"But I thought you hated me?" I said, still horrified. "You *told* me you hated me! You told the crew you hated me!"

"That's the problem. I think I liked you *too* much." she said.

"Bullshit," I wasn't buying this. "Look, I've been very nice to you. Whatever you're doing right now, I don't deserve it. I haven't done a damn thing wrong to you."

"You don't believe me?" she pouted again, stepping toward me. "You don't believe I'm infatuated with you?"

"No, I sure as hell don't," I said resolutely, stepping backwards into the mast.

But then an odd thing happened. She started to get red in the face. Somewhere under that perfectly controlled persona a *real* emotion was forming. This might be one of the first non-rehearsed displays I'd ever seen from her. Anger, sadness, possibly even embarrassment? Whatever emotion was about to show, it was giving me a hint of pity.

"All I've been doing is trying to get your attention! So you'd *notice* me," she said with forced evenness, but her voice started to crack a little.

I stared blankly at her for a second. Honestly, the pause was me asking myself, *Is this her best performance yet, or is this real?*

"Well, you've sure as hell got my attention now!" I said "You've had most of my attention since Arcot! I mean, what the hell do you want from me?" I asked, but that was a mistake! She stepped in close again, slipping her arms under my open great coat and around my waist, and I saw her eyes close and her face came close again.

"Whoa, whoa, whoa!" I said, "Now hold on!" I held her back.

That's when the eggshell broke.

Her face went red, her eyes squinted, and in a constrained voice she said, "Fine." In that "*fine*" was a threat, and I already knew she could deliver. She stomped below deck. How someone so small can cast such a cloud of poison and anger around her, I'll never know.

Later that night I wrote the beginnings of some lyrics in my journal:

The Ballad of Captain Robert

Captain Robert took his men

And flew to Prague and back again

Some fell off, some dropped dead

And some put bullets through their heads

A skeleton crew is what came back

Who lived through mutiny, plague and flak

Strong and callused, brave and tired

All those who could stay inspired

Captain Robert took his ship

To Beijing and to Mozambique
Stir crazy or in irons he clapped them
One of them tried to kiss the captain
A skeleton crew is what came back
Who lived through mutiny, plague and flak
Strong and calloused, brave and tired
All those who could stay inspired

I didn't see her again for a week. We tied off just above a forest a couple miles outside a foggy little fishing town, a couple hours north of London, and as the crew made quiet repairs I didn't spot her once.

Occasionally, I was given confused hints from the crew that "Lilith stormed in asking about empty crates. I told her to talk to you, cap'n." Or, "When's Lilith going to return my wrenches? The girl's had'em for a week." In retrospect, I should have looked into these things, but I was so relieved to have her out of my hair, I did nothing.

A STOLEN MONSTER

We were rested and prepared for our next mission. I stood at the wheel, once again with Daniel over my shoulder. We had spent the week laying plans for our biggest task yet, to take down the biggest villain I had ever heard of.

The ship was even more "bolted down" than before. With each jump through time, it seemed more things broke loose, so we kept tying more and more down in the hopes to not emerge in a dangling mess. The problem was that some of the damage was becoming structural, and all the ropes in the world weren't going to hold together the cracked beams running though the center of the hull. However, we'd gotten so mindlessly confident with our ability to make do, we risked it again and again.

"Hit the switch!" I yelled into the horn. In a moment, I felt the sinking feeling, and the whole room started an arrhythmic rumbling. That was new. My ears popped, this time incredibly painfully! Without thinking, I let go of the wheels to grab at my ears, and the ship lunged like we'd hit the side of a mountain!

I flew off my feet and slid across the floor, smashing into the stained-glass window and shattering several panels that embedded themselves in my face and hands.

The entire room, in fact, the entire gondola then began to swing back the other direction. Daniel grabbed the wheel in my absence. I could see blood dripping from his ears down the side of his cheeks. He had the amazingly useful skill of being able to ignore pain until after a battle was over.

As the gondola reached the far side of its swing, I could hear ropes outside *twang*, and *snap*, and the cabin dropped a foot or more, sending books and maps fluttering through the air. It seemed some vital support lanyards had broken free, and now the whole ship was a foot or two off-kilter.

Soon things settled down, and I stood up. Daniel flashed me a raised eyebrow to say, "Not good!" He tied off the wheel and we staggered out on deck, hands to our ears, to get our position.

It was cold. Cold as death, and the cuts on my face and hands burned. The deck of the *Ophelia* hung slightly angled, and as the other sailors emerged they walked cautiously and commented to each other in the soft worried tones you whisper at someone's deathbed.

I pointed my glass downward and scanned across pine trees, little rivers, a quaint European house with a steep roof, and a handmade fence with a horse tied to it. Past the house were green fields, and roads, sheep, a brand new "vintage" automobile, a grain silo, and…

Daniel tapped my shoulder, and I heard a terrifying sound; Propellers. I raised and focused my glass and I saw fighter planes! My heart dropped.

Thirty or more World War II fighter planes were flying parallel to us a couple miles to port, each sporting the insignia of the Luftwaffe. They appeared to be escorting two massive zeppelins.

We'd made a mistake. Actually, I had made a mistake, a big one. I had taken on our greatest goal: to stop Hitler and his genocide during World War II. We'd been fairly successful up until now, and I had gotten cocky. When we planned this mission, I didn't account for the fact that this war took place fifty years *after* the H.M.S. *Ophelia* had been built. It all seemed like ancient history, from my perspective.

But we'd been winning because we always had superior technology. Now we were essentially in the future compared to when the ship was built. We were antiquated. I had overlooked the fact that the German army at this point was massive, incredibly strong, and unbelievably high tech by Victorian standards. Most importantly, I had overlooked the fact that they had an actual air force.

"What in god's name is that!!!" yelled one of the crew, as the cloud of fighter planes altered course and headed towards us.

"That's trouble" I muttered back. *That's the end of us all!* Is what I wanted to say, but luckily I didn't say it out loud. I did however start yelling orders, "Turn the ship to port, head into those fighter planes...aircraft...airplanes... head *toward* them! Drop the sails! Propellers on full!" We couldn't outrun them, but if we headed into them they would have less time to shoot at us before they passed us. Running would only give them a more vulnerable target.

The *Ophelia* started a steep turn, but there was another snap of cables. The deck dropped down another two feet askew, and the sudden pitch bounced two crewmen overboard and knocked several others to the deck. This ship was already falling apart, and the fighters hadn't even gotten to us yet.

"Get the cannon ready!" I yelled. "Tie down those posts, and bring in the mainsails!" This was not going to be easy, if it worked at all. Crewmen were running, and climbing ropes and yelling, and tossing ropes.

In the commotion, I grabbed at Tanner's coat, and yelled over the now roaring wind, "Get to the map room. Tell the doctor to start his calculations. We need to get the hell out of here!"

"Those calculations typically take him a full day, and the doctor has been feeling very poorly. We need to make do without him," Tanner declared. He also glanced over my shoulder, and I saw him make eye contact with Lilith, who then went below deck.

I refused to let my mind spend a second on that, and yelled, "He'll die with the rest of us if he doesn't pull this off! Go!" I yelled, and Tanner bolted below deck.

The Luftwaffe's first pass was not a scouting run. This was the very heart of the war (*brilliant* timing, on my part) and we were in German airspace.

There were no warning shots. There was no signal for us to turn around. The first greeting we got was an unmerciful pelting from at least six guns. The wood of the front railings burst like popcorn, spraying the crew with wood chips before filling them with lead. Many men were cut in half before the rest dove to the decks.

A dozen friends died before we had a chance to shoot back.

As the planes whipped past, our cannons erupted a response! The sides of the Ophelia were wreathed in smoke and flames, but not a single shot hit its mark. Shooting planes with swivel-mounted cannon was futile.

Ophelia was starting to veer off course now, so as soon as the last of the planes had passed, I ran forward to the wheel. The acting pilot was among the first to be killed as the planes passed, so I grabbed what was left of the wheel. There was a stinging in my cheeks, and I reached up and felt the blood and glass that was still there from the stained-glass window I flew through just minutes before. I could feel the hot stickiness of blood running down my neck. Pulling on the Elevator Wheel brought us up to the height of the Zeppelins. They were flying directly toward us, parallel to one another and about one hundred feet apart.

Just before they reached us I turned off our starboard propeller. "Tell the gunners to hold their fire, and wait for my signal!" I yelled, and then threw the starboard propeller into reverse.

Ophelia began a quick pivot just as the Zeppelins started to pass us. When they were evenly on both sides, I slowly reversed the starboard propeller again, and we took a course matching theirs. The plan here was simple enough, if it worked. We could hold position between them and this would make it very difficult for the fighter planes to get to us without hitting their own airships. This was not a course to victory. I was only stalling.

Ophelia was not a small craft, and the distance between us and the other airships was only thirty or so feet. Of course, it would be easy enough for them to alter course and leave us exposed, but this was the best I could come up with on such short notice.

But they didn't alter course.

"Should we fire, Cap'n?" Mongrel asked, nervously making eye contact with the German pilot.

"For god's sake, no!" answered Daniel, who understood the whole plan. "They are our cover. Just wait. Let's see what they do."

They did nothing. They continued their course for a full three minutes, which seemed like an eternity. During this time some of the fighter planes had swung around, and took up a similar course just outside our little ménage à trois.

Then the Luftwaffe made their move. Over the tops of the airships they came, the bombers, and we were sandwiched between these hulking giants! There was no escaping. Our only possible course was down, and that would not be an escape.

I panicked and threw the propellers into reverse, hoping to

drop enough speed to avoid the bombs as they fell. Instantly there was a grating metal sound and the props pivoted sickeningly, and then froze at odd angles.

"Shit, shit, shit! Robert, what the hell have you done!" yelled Daniel, as he ran up to me. "This is not goo..." he started to say, but was interrupted by whistling sounds from overhead.

The bombs were away.

I heard a large explosion, and shockwaves rippled around the edges of our airbags like ripples in still water.

"FIRE!" I yelled as the second bomb hit. Ropes that held our massive gondola to the airbag were cascading around us, burning and smoking as they fell.

Our cannons fired, and the starboard Zeppelin burst into flames! In seconds the entire airbag was ignited. They didn't expect that. It was the first time a ten pounder ever plugged into the side of a hydrogen filled zeppelin. Thankfully, we were not getting lift from hydrogen, or we would have been a fireball too!

But it was too late, more ropes snapped, and with a huge drop that sent our sailors falling overboard, the port side of our gondola broke free and fell. Everyone still on deck slid into the port railing, which now hung at the bottom of a forty-five degree inclination. Cannon, crates, and casks slid on top or around them, breaking railings, and sailors. Half the deck crew plunged over the railing, and fell to their death.

Above us, the airbag was rolling up and away! After a second, however, the gondola stopped falling, and the airbag stopped climbing with a massive jerk. The gondola now hung from what was once the top of *Ophelia's* airbag, but which was upside-down and burning on the bottom where the bombs had hit when it was upright. The gondola was tied only at one side, and dangled defeated at a severe angle.

Then we heard more whistling.

I felt a massive rush of fear, of anxiety, and then my ears popped.

Instantly clouds formed around us, lightning flashed, and the sky was black. Wind hit us, and we started to swing wildly but something crashed into the side of the gondola.

Trees! Pine trees were tangled with the bottom of the ship, and were slowly rising as we dropped flaccid to the ground.

As soon as my feet touched the pine-needled floor, I ran to the dangling rigging and tied her off. Other sailors were doing the same, and others still were helping the injured to the ground, helping falling sailors up off the forest floor.

After things had been secured, Daniel and I climbed back on board the angled ship, and made our way below deck. There were unconscious and wounded sailors everywhere piled among the debris.

We made our way to the map room, and found Tanner, drenched in blood from a gash in the side of his head. He was laying on the floor holding the frail and unconscious Calgori.

Tears of guilt filled my eyes.

Tanner looked up. "Robert," he said slowly, "I think I made a mistake. I think I should have left with..." but his voice trailed off.

I helped Daniel pick the doctor's small body off the floor, and we did our best to gingerly move him from the cabin, and down the hall. He was disturbingly light, and frail-feeling. We eventually got him to the ground, and laid him on several coats by a fire. In a few hours we had set up a makeshift camp on the forest floor. We had no idea where, or when, we were, but it was easy to see there were very few of us left.

All night we nursed the wounded, or slept. In the morning we buried the sailors that didn't survive the night.

But that evening the doctor woke, and those remaining exhaled in relief.

It turns out Doctor Calgori had taken us fifty-five years back from where we experienced our fantastic defeat. In his rush, the doctor had miscalculated and we re-emerged only a few feet from the ground. It was a dangerous error, but it also happened to save our lives. Fifty feet lower, and we would have emerged underground, but as luck had it, we emerged close enough to avoid falling to our deaths as the deflated and burning airbag finally gave up.

"I knew the likelihood of miscalculation was great, and typically I would have erred on the side of more altitude, not less, but considering the state our ship was in, we needed to get her down before she let go of us," Calorgi said laboriously. "Still, I got the date right I think!"

Over the next few days, we laid more plans, and tried to figure out what had gone wrong. Those left who felt like talking were gathered around the fire: myself, Daniel, Calgori, Kristina. Tanner had nothing to say and stayed in his tent a few feet from the fire, and nobody had seen Lilith since that glance I caught on deck.

"But even given the fact that they had an air force," I started to ask, "Why did we *arrive* broken? I mean, that was the worst jump we've made! It should have been the most stable, but the ship was practically destroyed before we arrived!"

Calgori drew a rasping breath. "That is because we were sabotaged. After the jump through time, as you all ran on deck, I was busy as a bee below deck trying to figure out what caused the damage. It would appear one of the chromatic orbs that helps us travel through time had been removed. It's a mid-ship orb, not easily seen, so no one noticed it was missing. With this gone, our jump was off balance, and it caused an amazing amount of stress." The doctor paused. "This orb was also one that could be used on its own, if wired correctly, and all the piping and wiring to it had been carefully removed as well." The doctor paused "Someone who knew a lot about our ship seems to have taken it to use themselves."

Daniel gave a sharp look to Kristina, and then to me. Tanner left his tent and headed off into the trees without a word.

"Wait, you're saying one of our own crew took a part of our engine? Why would they do that? Wouldn't they be risking their own lives?" I asked.

"Not if they left the ship before we activated the Chrononautilus," Calgori answered.

Daniel spoke up, "If that's the case, then whoever it is, they're behind us, and we can…"

"Technically," Calgori interrupted, "they are ahead of us by forty or so years."

"Fine, ahead of us. The question is, what do we do now?" Daniel continued.

"We have a multitude of options," Calgori said. "I believe

we are now very near the time when our mission started. In fact, less then twenty years prior to the *Ophelia's* first journey through time. This is around the time I first started building the large scale Chrononautilus for the Royal Navy. Which means I think I can…HAH haha!" The doctor started chuckling.

I looked at him, questioning, and he answered, "When I first started my large-scale constructions, spare parts started to become scarce. I had an account at several places where I ordered things like the glass orbs construction, or the rare gasses I used. But I regularly found the bill far higher then I expected, and often found certain items would inexplicably sell out before I could get my hands on them."

He sat up looking almost playfully amused, and took a long draft of tea before continuing "I was certain this was because some competing scientist was on the verge of discovering the same technique I was to use. It turns out I was only partially correct. I believe the scientist I was competing with was me!"

"I don't understand," Kristina stated.

"If I can get to a telegram office," Calgori said "I can use my accounts the Navy has established for me to order replacement parts for the *Ophelia*! I can order from the same sources, I remember them well, and have them delivered here. Which explains why I will have trouble ordering them in my office in Whitby over the next few years! The other doctor I was competing with is myself, here and now!"

"Well, hell, if you can send a telegram to your supply houses, can you send a note to yourself that tells me not to go to Germany?" I asked half-joking, not sure what his answer would be.

"I'm not sure I would deliver that to you, even if I did. You have done a lot of good for a lot of people with your wild antics through time, even if many of our crew lost their lives on this mission. I'm not sure it'd be a good idea to tamper with your rashness." He paused, and his face went through a series of quick expressions, which always indicated he was in speedy thought. He continued then more quietly, as if to himself, "But perhaps a simplified application of the *Chrononautilus Effect* could be put into a device for sending notes. I will send myself a note to create a device called a...Chronofax? Ooo, that's good. A *Chronofax*." He said, savoring the word.

I said nothing. Now I was confused. Had Calgori just thought of inventing the device that had been in my family for years, or was he again showing signs of dementia, and had forgotten this very device had sat in my cabin this entire journey? Surly *he's* seen it before? In fact, I assumed he had placed it there.

Daniel then got us back to task, "Then we have a plan for the repairing of the *Ophelia*. What about the mission at hand?"

"Wait, I think I have an idea," I said, "How old was Adolf Hitler when he was in power? Specifically, how old would he be right now?"

April 20, 1889, at precisely 5:45 in the evening, a black motorcycle and sidecar, virtually indistinguishable from bikes that would be used by the German armies some thirty years later, pulled onto the crushed gravel driveway of *Gasthof zum Pommer,* an inn in *Braunau Am Inn, Austria–Hungary.*

A girl in her mid twenties un-straddled the bike, removed her leather jacket and leather helmet, pinned her hair under a small wedge shaped nurse's hat, and picked up a stack of fresh towels from the side car. She walked slowly to the front doors–she was a bit road-sore from her travels–and went in. She had a fresh cut down one thigh, but her skirt nearly hid it.

Once inside, it was easy to know where she was going. At the bottom of the stairs and across from the front bell-desk was a group of men smoking cigars around a little table while their companion paced nervously. The men made good-natured jokes and taunts to him.

The men at the table looked up to see the leggy blond nurse enter, "*Guten Tag, Fräulein, sind Sie hier, um mit dem Baby zu helfen?*"

"*Was denken Sie?*" she replied in an annoyed but flirtatious tone.

Up the stairs she went and into the nursery. There a bald and bespectacled man was taking off his gloves, while another nurse washed a screaming newborn. The mother slept.

"Wer sind Sie?" the nurse asked Kristina as she entered, which means roughly "Who are you?"

Kristina then explained that their uncle had sent her because she had delivered his children. She wasn't supposed to replace the nurse, but simply help, and please don't send her away, she hadn't worked in a month.

"Fine, then you can finish cleaning this brat while I have a piss." And the nurse stormed out.

When she'd left, Kristina locked the door and picked up the baby. She stood over the sleeping mother for a moment with a look of pity "Believe me, this will be less painful. You'll never know what this baby would grow up to become."

And with that Kristina climbed out the window and down the trellis, and headed back to her motorcycle. She set baby

Adolf in the sidecar, and kick-started the bike. As she sped out of driveway she thought, *...and that was the end of the Third Reich. I wonder what this child will become being raised on an airship amongst pirates?* It had to be better the what he would have otherwise become...right?

ENTROPY

During Kristina's "road trip", the rest of us made camp in the forest. It was a small camp of makeshift tents, many from old sails, on the cold, wet, pine needle floor, deep in the heart of the Black Forest, in Germany. We pulled timber from the ship that was too shattered and loose to remain, and stacked it around the tents. We deflated the huge gas bag, and found that even deflated it was massive, so we covered it with countless bushes and tree branches in the hope of making it less noticeable. Luckily, at this time in history there was almost no air travel, so we weren't likely to be spotted. This forest was vast, and mostly deserted. We had a good hiding place.

Our days were filled with hard and bitter work, pulling apart the ship in the effort to take a tally on how much damage was done, and preparing to replace it with undamaged lumber.

On one of his many walks through the woods, Tanner came across an old, abandoned church. A fire had burnt away a large part of the chapel, but there was still plenty of old wood that was salvageable. These ancient timbers were beautifully carved. These ornate beams were added to the already culturally eclectic mix of materials the *Ophelia* had bolted on as we were forced to repair her through the ages. Colored glass windows and lanterns from Persia, tooled leather and silks from Thailand and India, old submarine parts from the auto wrecking yard in Iowa. Every repair job was making her more a work of art than a weapon of war.

We also, unfortunately, learned some lessons. We learned that just because a man was a strong sailor did not mean he could wield a hammer. Calgori also learned we only had two hammers. It was odd, the doctor was the best builder among us. Anything he worked on came out flush, tightly mounted, and polished. Although he looked like he could barely walk, and he was having trouble remembering *why* we were here working on this, he could swing a hammer or lift the end of a beam as if he were a man in his thirties, not a man in his late eighties.

At times his will and his mind were so strong no one in the room dared dispute him. At other times, he was frail and sad, and looked riddled with guilt. I'm not sure what was going on behind those bushy eyebrows. He was fighting with some internal demons we didn't understand and he was fighting with his memory. One evening after a very hard day of work he called me father, and asked if he could go to bed. I said "yes", and no more. I didn't understand what was happening and wasn't feeling confident enough to interfere.

For repairs on the more delicate bits of machinery, as well as specific needs like canvas for sails and airbag, we ordered by telegram. I would drive Calgori to town in The Bandersnatch (that's the nickname we had given the little motorcycle and sidecar). He would place an order and give a credit account number. That account had been given to him by the English government for his original project of building the *Ophelia*. This made it less likely to attract suspicion. A few weeks later the supplies would arrive at the train station in town, and we would hire a local horse and cart to deliver the cargo to our camp.

One day we arrived at train station and found our supplies had not arrived.

In their place we found a letter. The doctor took it from the clean-cut young German postal employee, and read it with increasingly furrowed brow.

After reading it he uttered, "Damn it", and handed it to me. It read:

Much Esteemed Doctor,

It is my unfortunate duty to inform you your account is not being paid as per our original agreement.

Two disagreeable men came to my office to ask about your location. They made inquires as to why all your orders are being shipped to two separate locations. They also mentioned that you seemed to be nearly doubling the budget they expected from you.

Forgive me if I'm stepping outside of our business relationship, but we've been associates for years and I felt the responsibility to let you know your actions are being questioned.

With respect and concern,

~ Jonathan Farmor

When I had finished, the doctor was pacing, "...If they cut off supplies to us, we can make do. But if they cut off supplies to myself, well, there is no telling!" this he mumbled, then he turned to me. "Robert, we have to get to London! Immediately!" He pointed. "Wait, stop that mail boy, we have to send back a letter!"

The doctor flipped over the letter he had just read and, pulling a pen from his waistcoat, he wrote:

Jonathan,

Thank you for your letter. Please forward supplies to my Whitby address, COD. You may disregard my other orders for the time being.

I will go to London to speak with my financiers, and make sure your account is paid in full.

Much indebted,

Dr. L. Calgori

He folded this letter, put it back into its envelope, and handed it back to the mail boy. Turning to me he said, "It's important we get to London as fast as possible. I fear I made a mess of my accounts by ordering from this location. The English government has cut off my funding. If they stop sending supplies to the Dr. Calgori that is working in Whitby right now on the Chrononautilus, I won't be able to build the machine that got us here. What that will do to us as we are stranded here in the forest, I can't even guess."

He paused, and then swore in the most agitated tone I had yet heard from him. "Damn creditors! They will destroy the world one day, mark my words!"

We left the train station on a breakneck road trip west. I was not comfortable taking him on a long trip, since his health had not been improving, but he insisted angrily that this would be one of the most important trips we took together.

"Everything we've accomplished will be undone if we don't do this. We could be trapped here, or we may never have made it here, its impossible to tell!" he exclaimed.

So we left Germany, and drove through France towards the coast, driving all night long and into the morning, with me throttling the bike hard, and filling our small tank at the very rare petrol stations along the way. The sun rose the next morning and snow started to softly fall. I was cold, and sore from the small bike on the rough roads. As the doctor slept in the sidecar under his fur-collared herringbone coat he looked like he was on his deathbed. Old, pale, and frail beyond measure.

We took a ferry from Calais to Dover, and then drove west to London.

He woke and sat up just as the cycle wheels started bumping on the cobblestone streets of Old London. The building we were headed for was on the Thames, and if not for the attire of the people on the streets, or the vehicles we passed, I would swear I was in the modern London I remember from *my* childhood. The buildings of this neighborhood would remain untouched for hundreds of years.

All eyes were on me as I pulled the bike to a sputtering stop in front of the large stone stairs. Both the bike and I looked very out of place.

Calgori stepped from the sidecar into the snow, and pulled his clothes straight. "You need to make yourself scarce, Robert. You and your motorcycle are standing out in a place that does not appreciate things standing out. I will take care of this. Return for me in three hours. If I'm not here, I have gone to the pub for a drink. " He winked then, but he looked very frail as he turned and trudged up the steps.

The doctor told me what happened later. I was not there, but he told me about it in as much detail as he could, and I learned more from the people around him at the time I found him.

Doctor Calgori stormed into the office of Military Science and demanded to speak to his financier. He argued loudly, and made the desk-saddled soldier feel like a foolish enlisted man.

"I don't expect you to understand the processes that I must employ to accomplish this, son. I, in fact, don't expect you to fully understand what it is I am making, but luckily for us both you are not required to understand a damned thing! Your job is simply to make sure the bills get paid, and then report to your superiors that they have indeed been paid! If I ask that some supplies be sent to a master builder in Germany, who will then send the assembled parts on to me in Whitby, it is your job to simply pay the bill. You do not employ your small mind to the task of questioning my methods. Do we understand each other?"

For this tirade he stood taller than he had in years. He spoke louder than he had in years. His face grew red with rage, and he ignored the pounding in his head from the injuries he had been hiding for weeks.

When he was assured three times that all the bills would be paid on time from this point forward without question, he stormed out of the building.

And yet, the second the huge oak doors shut behind him, he sat down in the snow in a swoon. There he remained in the snow getting colder, staring at his legs and feet out in front of him, and he forgot himself entirely.

He knew the streets. The people felt familiar to him, and sitting on these steps in the snow suddenly reminded him of waiting for his father outside his father's bank as a teenaged boy. He was getting colder still, and he thought, *I need to move around a bit and warm up. Father might still be hours yet, and I don't want to catch my death waiting for him. Perhaps Charlotte is working today and I could go see her.*

Charlotte was a girl of sixteen that worked at a pub only a few blocks from where his father worked. His father forbid the boy from seeing her, since she was not "of his station", but as a young man who liked to read Shakespeare, this only made the young barmaid all the more woo-able. So he stood clumsily, thinking to himself, *I sat too long, and my legs have fallen asleep*! And with that in his head, he hobbled carefully down the snowy stone steps.

He walked the seven blocks slower than a boy of eighteen should have, still thinking his legs were not responding due to the long sit on the cold stone. When he reached the corner of the pub, he was mortally tired.

And the pub wasn't there.

He was so tired now, he began to cry. He started to cross the street to see if the pub was on the other side, for it was now snowing so thickly that he could not see the other side of the road from where he stood.

Also, the motorcar speeding down the snowy cobblestones could not see him through the snow. It honked angrily and swerved, narrowly missing him, but knocking him to his hands and knees. As he tried to get back up, he slipped in horse manure and fell hard back into the filth of the street. His head hit the pavement too hard, but he didn't know the extent of it.

At this point a carriage driver reined his horse, narrowly stopping before hitting him. He helped the doctor up, and gently carried him to the side of the road, and said, "I hope you're near your destination, good sir. You look a mess!"

At that point Calgori saw a pub. Not the pub of his youth, but as he was not thinking clearly, this was close enough to feel a relief. "Yes, I believe I have. Thank you," he said to the driver, feeling embarrassed to have bothered him with his clumsiness.

And then *she* walked out of the pub! A delicate young beauty, with smooth golden hair. She was tiny and young, a girl of sixteen with cheeks smooth as peaches, and a clean fresh smile that told the world she had never known sorrow. She was just as he remembered her, as she pulled her new coat onto her tiny frame, buttoning the fur sash to cover her soft smooth neck. The girl of his youth could never have afforded such a coat, but the girl of his memories did.

He was so tired, and he ached all over from his fall, and the cold, and for other reasons he could not remember. The sight of her made him burst into tears, and he ran to her sobbing. Part of his mind felt the emptiness of years of living alone, but the conscious part of him just longed for the love of the girl of his youth. He had hunger and longing that had never been satisfied in the fifty years since he had last seen her.

When he reached her, he wrapped his muddy and horse-fouled arms around her and cried loudly into her shoulder. He wanted his tears of fear to be quenched by the love of this girl. Here was the comfort he had missed for a lifetime, and the beauty he hadn't seen in years of living alone in his workshop.

And then she screamed.

To her, a strange and hideously old man, with blood dripping down his wrinkled and repulsive face and arms had just run out of the street, and grabbed her. She was horrified by his hideous age, by his foul smell, by the look of terror and abandonment in his eyes. She screamed in terror of him.

A policeman from the corner who had watched this man stumble towards the pub saw the old man grab the young girl. He heard the girl scream, and leaped to her aid. As Calgori staggered back in terror of the girl's scream, the policeman clubbed him squarely in the head, cracking his weakened skull mortally.

I found him moments later. I had come when I heard the girl scream, and I held him in my lap as he bled out in the street. He told me how he had assured our finances for repairs, and he told me it was time for me to go back to my life, and go back for my friends. He told me to have children, while I still could, and love and be loved while it was still wanted of me.

Then he told me, "I am tired, father, and I miss mother."

And then he died in my arms.

I drove back in the snow, alone and crying. I told the crew what had happened, and many of them cried as well.

Over the next week, many of the original crew gave up. They were nearly back in their own time, and things had fallen apart to the point that putting them back together was simply too much for them.

Those left continued to finish the repairs the doctor had laid out for us, and at the end of three weeks, the ship was finished and ready to go, but there were only ten sailors left to fly it. Barely enough.

We discussed what was to come next. We were fairly sure the doctor had already set the map room for a return trip to 2006. The goal was to return before my small plane crashed into the *Ophelia*, and possibly save my band mates before they plummeted to their death that night.

After that, perhaps we'd return the remaining crew back to the times we had acquired them, or perhaps we'd all stay in 2006 – we weren't sure. We were not the least bit confident we could run the Chrononautilus without Calgori.

For the month that followed, we tied up all the loose ends, both literally and figuratively. The airbag had been patched, and filled, and the rigging had been re-tied with the ropes doubled in number.

We also found a home for the stolen baby. A small orphanage

about seventy-five miles southeast of us was run by Catholic nuns. They seemed both strict and loving. That alone seemed a combination that would keep this child from developing into the monster he otherwise would have become. A child raised by one set of parents, molded by them, and instilled with the morality they give will become a certain person. Remove their influences, the same child will become someone else.

In addition to this altering of the child's history, (and I refused to feel any guilt for this) an orphan in the 1900s simply would not have the resources to rise to become an evil dictator. He would not be afforded the best colleges. He would not spend his teen years and early twenties collecting a network of friends and connections in powerful places. He would end up with a much smaller, and less dangerous level of influence on his country.

Still, it did raise the moral question of "Can you condemn a baby for what he has not yet done?" Had this been any other child, this argument might have swayed us, but knowing who this baby would become, we decided to leave the child under the care of the holy sisters.

Finally, the calendar day caught up to the date of our original collision, and once again the ship was aloft, and ready for our final effort.

BOOK II

THE END OF DAYS

Once again we were hit with a sudden wind, pummeling our airbag and rigging like someone threw a switch and turned on a tornado. There was a horrible ripping sound, almost like some monstrous scream, followed by ropes twanging, and something huge and wooden finally tearing loose.

A second later, I saw a four foot section of carved wooden railing swinging towards me on a piece of lanyard, and smash through the starboard window of my cabin. That would take three days to fix, at least – but we were getting quick at rebuilding. Or we wouldn't bother to fix it, our adventure was just about at an end.

Soon the ship came to a swinging stop. Through the broken glass I could see it was a bright, clear sunny day. The wind was from momentum of the earth as we jumped through time. The actual weather here was hot, arid, and still.

I half-ran from my cabin, out onto the deck, snatching my spyglass as I did. On deck the rest of the crew was beginning to emerge from the portholes and stairways. I met up with Daniel at the railing. We extended our spy glasses in unison, and focused toward the ground.

Below us was a vast expanse of yellow grassland dissected by the remains of a freeway, cracked and ancient-looking in the hot sun. It was half-covered in dust and dirt, with bushes grown through the many cracks in it. About a mile up the road, in the direction we were heading, was a huge cloud of dust being kicked up by a caravan of vehicles. Massive semi-cabs, pulling three, four, and sometimes five different trailers behind them. The first trailer was a painted caravan-house like a huge gypsy wagon but with many floors and windows, the second was a flat bed trailer with greenhouses, and the third had a huge tank of water or fuel, and so on. They called these "hauls", and each family had at least one. This huge and colorful mobile town looked like someone crossed a victorian house with a circus train, overgrown and over-adorned.

The huge semi-trains were surrounded by smaller vehicles: rusty and haphazardly modified SUVs, small beat-up jeeps, odd handmade contraptions of varying design, a dozen motorcycles, and ten or so mounted horses and camels. The motorcycles and mounts were at the tail end, driving a herd of cattle, llamas, and a few dozen yards behind them were...

"Tigers? Are those tigers in the grass? Along the roadside slightly behind the caravan?" Daniel asked with excited concern.

"It looks like it. They seem to be stalking the herd!" I said.

At that moment there was a flash of movement. By the time I refocused my glass, it was over. A tiger - no a cheetah! - had left its hiding spot in the grass, and overtaken one of the bikers. The bike now lay on the ground, tires still spinning, and the black-leather-clad biker on his back kicking, with the body of the large cat extending from him, its face buried resolutely in the biker's neck. A few moments later the biker stopped kicking as other cheetahs gathered around and waited patiently for their turn to eat.

The other bikers and mounted riders started firing their rifles, not at the cats but into the air to drive the cattle faster.

"Not much we can do for him. He'll be dead before we can get there," Daniel said, lowering his glass.

The other cats had stopped pursuing the caravan, and were now gathering around the kill. Tigers, several lions, and at least six cheetahs waited to calm their hunger.

"Even still, let's catch up with that...what is it, a *wagon train*? Something is seriously wrong. If something like this occurred in

2006, a wagon train of semi-trucks driving cattle and attacked by a mixed pride of predatory cats, I think I would have heard about it! We should be over a major highway in Idaho, yet it looks like we're in the middle of the African Savanna, over a road abandoned for a hundred and fifty years! Besides, they've already spotted us by now, I'm sure. We didn't emerge in cloud cover, which means we are nowhere near the time and place of our original collision with the *Ophelia* as we had hoped."

Within a few minutes we had overtaken them. The occupants of the caravan were waving to us from the tops of their vehicles, as if we were a common sight! I descended by rope ladder onto one of the vehicles, where there stood a handful of young men with odd-looking but decorative long rifles and wide-bladed crescent swords. The men looked aggrieved, most likely due to the recent attack.

They stood around a white-bearded man, with an elaborate facial tattoo and decorative scarring. They were all dressed in colorful cloaks over baggy pants tucked into enormous boots, and they wore vests of leather and wool with ornate embroidery. Their skin color varied, ethnically they obviously came from many origins, yet culturally they were the same. The same style of cloths, the same piercings and long knotted hair, and henna tattoos on their necks, faces and hands...the same fire behind their eyes.

"I wish you'd arrived a few minutes earlier. A few shots from you might have scattered the beasts and saved our rider," said the old man in a gravelly and shaky voice that nevertheless inspired confidence.

"I'm sorry. We only just spotted you when the beast leaped," I said.

"Well, it's behind us now. Miles behind already, as are all

things in our past. Only one direction to look when you're moving, and that's forward." He paused here, possibly to make sure I had understood all the levels of meaning behind what he was saying.

Then he continued, "Your ship is beautiful – I've never seen anything like this. Where did you acquire it?" asked the bearded man. The elaborateness of his garb and his age told me he was in charge, and a man whose days of working with his hands were behind him. The younger men were obviously his guards.

Not having the foggiest clue where or when we were, I needed to not reveal something that I would regret later. I choose to speak honestly, but cryptically. "We are from a very long way off. You could say there is much time between our homeport and us."

The old man raised an eyebrow as if to say, "You think you are more clever than I am?" What he actually said was, "Fine, keep your secrets, I don't want 'em. I didn't mean to make you nervous, just making chit-chat. Shall we skip the chatter and get to it?"

"Okay," I said, feeling bested, and waiting to see where this was going.

He pulled out a small hand-written book, flipped open to a bookmarked page, and began to read aloud, "Let's see then, iodine, sewing needles - heavy, salt and any other spices you have, but especially salt. A big stew pot or something that will work as one. A couple dozen spoons. Light bulbs for this size fitting." Here he held up a broken flashlight that looked at least fifty years old. He went on, "Although I'm not sure cities would be allowed something like this?" Here he waited for me to respond.

"May I see your list?" I was starting to get the idea. "Yes, I have a lot of this, I'll see what we can spare. As I said, we're from a long ways off, and I'm sure we've got some things you might not be accustomed to seeing. Speaking of which, I'm primarily looking for news, and food, if you have some to spare. And a bit of lumber," I said, glancing up at a conspicuous hole in the belly of our ship. Sailors were looking down through the hole at us like tourists staring out the windows of a bus.

"I assumed about the food and lumber. Isn't that why you Skyborns always visit the Neobedouins? If you could grow and breed your own food and materials aloft, you'd have no reason to sell us medicines and what not, would you? But normally I'd be asking you for news. How long *have* you been aloft?"

"That...that has a complicated answer. Sorry, I'm not trying to be secretive, I'm just not sure how to answer that without telling a very long story. We've been aloft that long," I said in response to the annoyed look he gave me.

"Well, stay for the night. Tonight is our tether dance and we can talk then, and exchange news at the feast." Having had nothing but salted pork on crackers and a few mealy apples for the last two weeks, a feast sounded very good. I graciously accepted these colorful people's hospitality.

As the sun stained the side of our faces with orange light, the vehicles started to circle. A huge fire was made, food was cooked, and music was played within the circle. Our crew started to descend from our damaged airship to meet the nomads. Cushions were brought in to sit on, and low tables were brought out, and the food was laid on them.

Around the fire, young men and women, with bodies as lean and muscular as young horses, tied their painted bodies together with long leather ropes. Like this they danced around the fire, at times lifting each other from the ground, or hanging by their ropes from large posts that had been planted in the ground.

Wow, if we could just get some of these people to dance at our concerts, I thought to myself. *It's like we've come to the circus at the end of the world!*

At one point they untied the ropes, and dipped them in a pot of oil. Then they lit the ropes, and spun them, and continued their dance with the ropes on fire.

"I can tell this is your first time at a tether dance. It's the look on your face: you skyborn have to be so much more careful with fire then those of us who live down in the dust."

"It's truly impressive. Your tribe has very skilled. . . dancers?"

"True, dance, yes. But it's also a martial art. Perhaps not a stealthy one, but certainly effective at repelling man and beast."

As I contemplated this, I saw, out of the corner of my eye, Tanner walking toward the group of musicians, violin in hand. After a while, he traded his bowler hat to one of the nomads in exchange for one of their tribal-looking headpieces. It was something that looked like a Native-American headdress, had it been made out of belts and old pieces of machinery. I wondered whose belts they had been, and how they had come to be without a belt.

The old man spoke. "You hinted that you were from further away than we're used to. I've been watching your crew and I think I see. At first, I was concerned, as some of you seem very 'military'. My mind was set at ease, though, when I saw that you were not all Victorians at all."

At this he pointed to one of our riggers, who was photographing the dancers with a digital camera we picked up in my time. We had a few such devices with the crew, but not many since

Calgori never put much priority on freeing up a place to charge the devices. "You have devices that have not been legal since before Victor the First's reign, and that began long before my time! You try to hide them, but I see." He smiled cleverly and said in a quiet voice, "These things don't look old, or say, they don't look worn. Newer and cleaner than anything I've seen, and definitely illegal. That makes me curious." Here I must have been squirming, as he added, "You have nothing to fear here. We are the last of the free peoples and we would do nothing to take away your freedom. I also don't have any need to lead my tribe on a treasure hunt that would simply make them a greater target for the sky pirates, so I'm not trying to pry any map out of you." He thought for a moment before continuing. "Still, I think these are not artifacts from the ruined empire – they don't look *old*. Tell me your story, if you trust me, and I will give you news to calm the look of confusion on your face."

I think I did trust him. And, in fact, I now needed information from him as much as the *Ophelia's* original crew needed news from me when they found themselves stranded in a future they didn't understand. So I spoke, "You're right. We are not from here – in fact, I'm not even sure where we are. I would have said we were in the mid-west of the United States of America, based on the geography. But things are different; the colorfulness of your people, the wild animals, well, this seems like no place I've heard of before!"

"How could you have gotten so far, without seeing the route you took?" he asked. This was a clever question. Was he starting to guess at our story?

I sighed, "When I say we are not from here, I don't mean this place. I mean this time. The devices you have seen are not the most impressive things we have. On our ship is a machine that can take us through time. Most of my crew is from the 1900s, which is when the ship was built."

I sat quietly now to gauge his reaction. He said nothing, but stared intently, waiting for me to continue. "We've been journeying through time, trying to undo the 'wrongs' of humanity. We came to this time to try to stop the death of our friends, but I'm afraid we might have missed, since this is not the place we expected."

"This is a fascinating story you tell! Do I believe in Santa Claus, though we've all been told he's pretend, even when we meet him?" He looked very excited now, and I was *very* confused, "I wouldn't have believed it, except I have seen the things you have that should never have been. Nothing like that has been seen in two hundred years, if it ever was...and two hundred years ago they had nothing as clever, for things have not changed much since the 1950s, with the exception of things we've found out here in the wastes that have been abandoned by the Emperor."

"Wait...two hundred years since 1950!? How could that be!? If the year is 2150, how is it that you have not seen something as ordinary as a digital camera? Tell me the history of the world as you know it, tell me everything!"

"Well, it'll be hard to guess what you don't already know, but here is how things are. Emperor Victor the Third sits in an Eden he created, surrounded by beauty, comfort and technologies the rest of the world is not allowed. His castle is more fantastic than anything built before his time, or the time of his fathers, and their time has been very long."

"He loves animals more than people, and so he keeps his people caged, and saves the freedom of the outside world for the beasts. The cities he controls are vast filthy mazes, where he keeps every neighborhood behind a wall, and only lets his officers and members of the upper class travel between them.

"They police the cities, looking for anyone doing anything out of the ordinary. Anyone *progressing*. If he finds anyone doing anything new, especially making anything new, he locks them up in huge cages. In this way he assures that none of the people in his cities do anything different than they have for the last two hundred years. That's why we call the city folk neo-Victorians. They have not changed in fashion and technology since the Victorian times. Also, they are followers of the Emperor Victor. They strut around, preening in their tuxedoes, and top hats, and hooped gowns – fat, filthy and caged like pet peacocks."

"Around each city, of which there are perhaps three on the American content, is a huge wall. This wall keeps the people in. But occasionally people escape, and they do their best to live out here in 'the Wastelands'. WASTELANDS! HAH! That's what the Viccies call the lands of the free peoples. The lands of the Neobedouins and the Skyborn. But the real secret the city folk don't know is it's beautiful out here. Beautiful, and free.

"You see, the emperor loves the beasts more than any people, and so the beasts own the world between the cities. Here they graze, they hunt, they breed, they feed on each other, and they feed on any of the land-born tribes and our herds. The Skyborn stay aloft, like yourself, floating in ships that range in size from five-person homes, up to whole cities! They come down only to trade with us for food or other supplies which they can't make themselves.

"We Neobedouins don't go aloft, because that makes you a target. The Skyborn are always fighting with the airships of the Emperor, since they are easier to find. You see, a hundred years ago, when the Emperor first came to power, the world was a different place. The world was crowded, and filled with cities, and people, and too many cars jamming the roads at all times day and night. The first Emporer outlawed freedom in the false name of Environmentalism. He said it was for the Sake of the Planet. All were forced to live in his cities, and he outlawed living outside the cities. Since living outside is outlawed, only outlaws live outside!"

Here I interrupted with a question. "But, how did this Emperor come to power? How did the people of the world let him?"

"At first he became a president, back when there was that sort of thing. He said that presidents could not actually fix the world, because Congress prevented them from making changes. Congress, he said, was corrupt, and under control of corporations, so he had Congress eliminated. He then created laws to prevent him from having to give up his power at the end of his term, then he unified the nations of the world, all under his name. This was not always peacefully done, but often he had approval of his people. Create a common enemy, and people will approve of attacking them.

"Once he had total power, he began the depopulating. He told the people the world was becoming overfull. He said he had 'Seen the future first hand' and it's a nightmare of concrete mazes filled with angry, sickly people. He told whole towns he had to relocate them, for environmental reasons, to stop polluting, or stop killing some beast no one had heard about before then. He said he needed to relocate them. People were loaded onto huge trains and taken into the national parks he had been expanding. The people were then released, only to be fed upon by the beasts he had been breeding.

"With humans an unlimited food (there were nearly four billion people at that time) the beasts' numbers swelled, especially the predators, and feeding on so much human flesh made them grow immense and strong. Now lands between his cities are overrun with things that feed on men, since man has been the most abundant food source for the last one hundred years. Of course, that food source is now waning."

"His son, Emperor Victor the Second, upped the ante. He started bringing back species that had died out naturally. Prehistoric monsters that put lions and tigers to shame. Not all of these are predators – some Neobedouins pull their wagon trains with beasts that make elephants look petite. But there are also meat-eaters the size of a truck that wander the plains, and even our beast dancers are not skilled enough do anything but run from those nightmares."

We talked all night about these things. Eventually he got tired, and excused himself. I slept that night by the campfire, but before falling asleep I sketched these lyrics in my notebook:

The End Of Days

After our days and the fall of Man,
One day this will heal again.
Beasts crawl forth over desert clay,
And mankind will be nature's prey.
Ruined towns spring forth in vines,
Trees ... leaves ... fleet combine.
Humankind will have lost its sway,
The world again will be theirs one day.

Skeletons of rust reach for the sky,

Ruined empires of days gone by.
Dreams and lives buried in the sand,
The end of days will have been long planned.
Our children's children have passed away,
Their auspicious lives lost in the fray.
Carrion birds are all at play,
The world again will be theirs one day.

Nomadic tribes of the last of Man,
Pull their caravans across the sand.
Gypsy wives hold their children tight,
As the new superpower howls through the night.
Gods watch from above and wonder what went
wrong,
The entropy of what once was strong.
The survivors of Man stay up late to pray,
That the world again will be theirs one day.

AIRSHIP PIRATES

As we woke the next morning on our woolen sleeping mats around the smoldering fire, there was a great commotion. The Neobedouins were running around, yelling to each other through what I mistook for smoke. It was actually heavy fog, and I began to understand what they were all riled about. I saw the wheels and axles of one of their massive hauls disappearing into the low–lying clouds above us.

Leaping up, I grabbed the arm of a teenaged boy, and asked, "What's happening?"

"Pirates! Sky Pirates are stealing our food stores!" He was panicked, watching a three-storied haul disappearing into the fog.

Daniel stepped to my side as the boy quickly told us that some of the "Skyborn" (as he called them) would descend in thick early morning fog, hook the tribe's storage trucks, and just lift them away. If the pirates caught the tribe off guard, there wasn't anything the Neobedouins could do to stop them.

"Dammit, I thought we were the *only* airship pirates!" I joked to Daniel.

"Its not good to make assumptions, Captain," Daniel said with a slight grin.

"There is nothing to be done! We are lost!" said the young man. "Without our stores…"

"Maybe not completely. Daniel, don't *we* have an airship somewhere?" I asked.

"Why yes, Robert, I think we do. Shall we see if there's something that can be done about this?" he said.

"Oh yes, lets," I replied with mock mildness.

We ran for the ladders that hung under the *Ophelia* when we were moored to the ground, and we roused the crew as we ran. In a few minutes we were all on deck, and our ship hung in fog so thick we could barely see the airbag above us. Looking around, the crew appeared hungover, and in some cases still noticeably drunk. Nobody expected an early morning, and I had the feeling some of the crew had only just passed out from drink when this latest adventure began. My own head was still spinning a bit, I will admit.

"Lets get some altitude, and figure out where they've gone! Mongrel? Get the engines up to power!" I commanded.

"Aye, Cap'n!" he replied, and stomped below deck.

I strode up to the front helm, not in too much of a hurry as it would be a few minutes before the engines could supply me with enough power to get the ship in motion. As I walked, the wet fog clung heavily to my clothes and hair. I took my place at the wheel, and tried to peer through the murk. When the ropes had been pulled up, and the pressure gauges showed sufficient pressure, I pulled the elevator wheel. The ship slowly began to respond. It moved sluggishly, as if a million dewdrops were weighing her down.

Up we climbed, and further still. The clouds were much deeper then I originally assumed, and we were losing time. Soon our prey would be far away, and when we did get free of this cloud cover we'd have to find what direction to pursue them. When we finally broke free of the clouds and into early morning sunlight, we saw a grand spectacle of silver-pink sky above a sea of fluffy white. Here and there mesas poked up through the clouds, like islands, with little towns perched on top of them. Deep blue in the far distance to the west was a massive mountain range, and some of its peaks were also dotted with towns.

I scanned the sky around us for a sign of the other airship, and was confounded in a way I hadn't expected. There were at least twenty airships visible. Two near enough to see the color of their balloons, another half dozen scattered here and there at a distance that made them just pale blue silhouettes, and the remaining were specks on the horizon, flying into or out of the little mountain-top cities. Some were coming, some were going, some climbing, some descending to the little island mesa towns, each minding their own business on a typical morning for them. This was a new world, one in which we were no longer an amazing spectacle. We were now just part of the throng.

Off to our port side there was one massive and battered airship. It consisted of two huge cigar shaped balloons, under which hung the hull-equivalent of a nineteenth-century workhouse. This was four floors, square and unadorned, with broken windows and shutters. It was built of weather-stained wood that was once painted blue and white – but a couple of decades of poverty left more bare wood than paint. It was as shabby and depressing a construction as Dickens himself could have dreamed up, and it hung forlorn in the sky. Below the base of this sad structure were four or five massive ropes, tightly holding something large below and out of sight. This must be the pirate vessel, hiding the stolen haul in the clouds as they tried to escape unnoticed.

"Clever of them to try to sneak off low like that, hoping we'll take pursuit of someone else. You'll notice they aren't even at half speed. They are putting on quite an act!" I said to the crew around me. I pulled the yellyphone up to my mouth, adjusted a ring on it that allowed it to address the whole ship, and I spoke, "Load the cannons, and prepare for battle! We are going after that behemoth to port. Daniel, prepare a boarding party!"

I gave the wheel a spin, and the ship swung around. Below deck I could hear boots running, and men barking instructions and confirmations at each other. They would be loading powder, stacking shot, and rolling the huge guns into open hatches. The routine of combat was old hat to us now, and cockiness once again swam through our heads.

"Cannons to port, men. We'll be passing on her starboard side," I said. I throttled up the props, and our engines raised pitch. Soon we were closing on the ship like a shark confidently closing on a swimmer, the clouds breaking on our bow like waves in the sea. Soon our bow was even with her stern. We were fifty yards to starboard, and we watched her shutters closing in preparation for battle. When we were even, I gave the command, "Give her a volley! Half-guns warning, we don't want her to burn and fall." A few of our cannons blazed, and the shot found its mark. One entered a window in an unsatisfyingly easy manner. Another hit the balloon, and literally bounced off. They weren't exploding shot, just heavy balls, that balloon must be made of some impressively thick canvas! Another two shots found wood, and left gaping holes. Through the holes, I could see small figures running further into the ship. *That's odd,* I thought. *Little pirates? Does that make it easier to fly or something?*

"Reload, and hold!" I commanded. They weren't returning fire. Perhaps they were thieves, but not pirates? They steal, but aren't equipped for aerial combat? It was as likely as anything else, this *was* a foreign world to us.

Daniel walked up to me. "Let's tie her up, and go aboard. I don't think they've got much on us."

"I agree," I said, turned and yelled, "Fire grappling!" There were a dozen whistling sounds, as our huge steel darts, attached to heavy lanyards, flew the distance between our ships and found easy purchase in the increasingly frail sides of our prey. After the grappling fire, the next sound was the *ching, ching, ching* of huge shipboard ratchets being wound, pulling us closer to our prey.

When we were close enough that our airbags touched, our hulls were still a good thirty feet away from each other. A boarding party of about ten of our crew, armed with both swords and pistols, single- or double-shot types, from the various eras we've been spending our time in.

I know the swords must seem ridiculously romantic, like a caricature of movie pirates, but the truth was much more practical. Whenever we changed times it became very difficult to find ammunition to fit our pistols. The old-style pistols could use hand-forged bullets, but that was difficult and those guns were horribly inaccurate. For a while we got used to throwing away guns as soon as they ran out of ammo, since we rarely got the chance to acquire the correct bullets again.

However, as primitive as it might sound to you reading this, three-feet of sharpened steel is always effective. They never run out of bullets. These swords were not like the replicas you've handled in mall smoke shops, clumsy, rattling, duller than butter knives. Imagine the best chef's knife, able to slice paper without ripping it. Able to make a two-millimeter, transparent slice of an over-ripe tomato (or the same from an incautious finger holding that tomato). Able to cleave a heavy ham-bone with one hard swing. Now imagine that razor-sharp blade is three feet long. Better then a one-shot pistol, and three bullets in your pocket, right?

So with swords drawn we leaped, tethered only by the long leather straps we kept tied to the furthest edge of our airbag.

Through the air we swung, thousands of unknown feet between us and the ground. Down to the bottom of our arc, then back up, until a sudden release, and our boots hit deck! There we all stood on the other ship, while I tried not to show the pride I felt at not having fallen to my death, or worse, bounced and swung back. (This hadn't happened to me, but I've seen sailors swing back and forth, and ultimately end up dangling in the middle, lacking the momentum to reach either ship. If they lived through the battle, they had an even harder time living with the embarrassment.)

We were standing on a deck that ran like a porch around the middle of the hull. Everything here was dingy old wood. Rotting and in ill-repair, like an old school-yard fence that had stood too long after the school was abandoned. Oddly, there was nobody to greet us. No bold crew of pirate-thieves to fend us off.

"It's a trap, Cap'n!" Mongrel growled. "Let's go in and wake 'em up!" For anybody but Mongrel, these two statements would contradict each other, but he was the type that liked to take things head-on. He was six feet of scabs, built like a leather oak tree, so he could take the brunt of a misstep in stride. He stepped toward the nearest doorways, but before we could open them we were engaged!

Leaping from windows before us came men. Or say, young men, brandishing swords. The narrowness of the walkway meant only one of our large pirates could fight them at once, although our narrow opponents had no trouble finding room to stand three abreast. They had neither strong thrusts, nor parries, and it was easy to push all three back, even though it was only me fighting with them. In the blinding sun light above the clouds, I couldn't get a good look at them.

While I fenced with them, the windows above us opened, and we were splashed with water! The water was neither hot nor cold, so it didn't do more then surprise us. There were also books, and little pieces of wood, puzzle pieces, and sticks thrown on our heads. Again, it didn't hurt, it was just – strange! Finally, I disarmed one of the young men, kicked another to the ground, and all three ran through the large doors that had opened behind them.

We followed them in. It was much darker inside, and as our eyes grew accustomed to lack of light I stepped on something soft. Bending down, I picked up a small rag doll.

"Seriously, what the fu…." I started to say, when I was interrupted by the sound of gun fire! Specifically, machine gun fire. We jumped back outside–miraculously nobody had been hit–and we stood around the corner, out of harm's way.

The gun fire stopped, and an equally abrasive voice came from around the corner, "I'm afraid you're out of luck," said the gravelly voice of a lady in her sixties, who sounded like she'd spent her last thirty years making very hard choices. "We've got nothing much left to steal, so I'm afraid you've wasted your shots on us. Food's nearly out, too, and we don't carry any money," she said, "and honestly you should be ashamed of yourself fighting with children!"

Children? What the hell is going on? I was beginning to think we'd got another case of our heroics backfiring.

"I'm not here to take anything that's yours. I just want the haul you stole this morning!" I replied.

"It's like I said," she replied, "You're wasting your time, pirate. These children didn't steal any haul this morning," she said with a pitying laugh. "This morning we were moored at Isla Aether. We haven't hardly left port when you started hunting us down like we were a Navy cargo ship. A silly, pointless thing to do, but you're not the first silly pointless pirate to think you were going to find hidden treasure here. Now, lay down those kitchen knives, before I turn you into Swiss cheese!"

Wow. This wasn't some strange *Lord Of The Flies* airship crew. It was a goddamn orphanage in the sky! *Aw, what the hell,* I thought. This was painfully embarrassing.

I quickly considered my options. At this point we could:

A: Run at her with swords drawn, and get a face full of post-apocalyptic tommy gun.

B: Run back to our tethers, and try to swing back to the *Ophelia*, while likely getting shot in the back by the afore mentioned post-apocalyptic tommy gun.

C: Command the gunners aboard the Ophelia to fire, who'd possibly hit us, but definitely making the ship on which we stood less flightworthy.

Or D: Lay down our swords and pistols, and accept our embarrassing fate.

I chose D. I now firmly believed we were way off-target, so we laid down our weapons.

There stood a comical, yet intimidating sight. Ten or more small to teenage boys and girls, surrounding one Catholic nun. She was old and tanned like saddle leather, grim-faced, and pointing a sling-mounted six-barreled repeater! This was one tough-ass grandma. If she had had whiskers and a cigar in her mouth, it would have not surprised me. She spoke condescendingly to us from under her tattered but clean habit. "Now, explain to me again why you are putting holes in my orphanage."

"Yeah, about that," I stammered. "Last night we made friends with a caravan tribe. Neobedouins. This morning as we awoke someone had air lifted one of their supply trucks. We were trying to recover them, when we saw you carrying off something heavy, obscured in the clouds."

"Yup," she laughed. "It's like I thought. You guys are idiots." That hurt. "Get out of my school, while I'm still laughing at you," she said.

We did as we were told. Back to the railing, and over we swung.

Later that week I sketched out these lyrics in my notebook:

Airship Pirates
Our fire's high and the airbag's tight
Food's low but the skies are bright
Props spinning all through the night
We're low on cash but we'd seen another target
Goggles down and the cannons up
My blood starts pumping as I drain my cup
I give the wheel a spin and I turn this girl around
We're way above ground but we're closed in on our target

Flying jib is filled with air
East India ships filled with despair
We even up, her broadsides bare
Our cannons flair but it's just a show of muscle
Steady on, she doesn't need to burn
She tries to flee and she tries to turn
Grappling fire, we latch her hull
She's starting to roll, but we've got her on a

leash

With a crew of drunken pilots
We're the only airship pirates
We're full of hot air and we're starting to rise
We're the terror of the skies, but a danger to
ourselves now

Expendable crew starts to reel her in
Our swords are sharpened and we're ready to sin
I'm three miles up, we're about to swing aboard
My tether's made of leather so I'm not about to
fall here

A swish of air and my boots hit deck
No cash, no fuel, no not a speck
Our grapeshot's made this bird a wreck
And a glance below deck shows a crew of nuns
and orphans!

Chorus
With a crew of drunken pilots
We're the only airship pirates
We're full of hot air and we're starting to rise
We're the terror of the skies, but a danger to
ourselves.

A Minor Redemption

When the boarding party climbed over the railings of the *HMS Ophelia*, we were greeted by baffled looks. "What happened? We heard a lot of gun fire, are you okay?"

"We're fine. Wrong ship is all," I mumbled, avoiding eye contact with anybody. I strode to the aft deck and pulled open my spyglass while the rest of the boarding party explained to the crew what had happened. As Daniel explained the situation I tried not to think the stifled laughter was at my expense.

Gazing through my tarnished scope I could see what I thought we were looking for. There was a familiar cigar shaped gasbag and gondola combination – very similar to the *Ophelia's* design – hoisting the brightly painted gypsy haul that had been lifted from the Neobedouins camp as we slept this morning. We had been looking in the wrong direction.

"Come about!" I yelled to the acting pilot, as I ran forward to the helm. And I added to the crew, "To the guns! Prepare for battle!" And once again the crew was in motion. My ears were filled with the *clop-clop* of heavy boots, the sound of the rigging straining as the ship came about, and the now wind-muffled sounds of men yelling to each other.

The deck was still moist with dew, but I was now warm with my morning's exertions, and the cool breeze worked wonders to drive the embarrassment of our botched attack from my mind.

I took the wheel from the acting pilot, and throttled up the props. It appeared that our new prey was flying by wind power alone, so catching them would be no problem. In fact, trouble would not begin until we came within firing range. At that point, we would be put to the test. This would be our first combat against another airship that had actually been outfitted for aerial combat. Until recently all our fights had been ground targets or sea targets, and we always held a huge advantage over them.

Their shots had gravity working against them, whereas I could practically drop my boot over the railing and expect at least someone would get hurt.

There was also the problem of the cargo we were trying to recapture. A ten-ton, three-story, semi-truck sized haul hanging by ropes six thousand feet above the ground did not sound like an easy grab, but I was formulating a plan. Still, with all our misadventures lately, I was not walking into this without some apprehension.

"So, what's the plan, Captain?" Daniel asked. *Possibly a touch sarcastically?* I wondered.

Now, the picture in my head of how the plan was to work made sense. It would work, but it did sound like things might get a little shaky, and it wouldn't work if the whole crew was doubting me while we tried it. I decided not to divulge the details just yet, since the crew still lacked confidence in me, so I said, "We'll just go up there and get'em!"

"Get'em? That's your whole plan?"

"Hey, have a little faith!" I said, not sure if I did.

"Because that's been working so great up until this point?" Daniel retorted, but our banter was cut short by a sound. The aft of our prey became obscured by four little puffs of gray smoke, followed by a muffled *POOM! POOM! POOM! POOM!* as the sound reached us. From these little clouds came four trails of smoke stretching out to our port side - obviously missing us. Each tendril of gray smoke was tipped with something spinning that glinted in the morning sun, and each emitted a strange mechanical whirring sound. The sound was comical. They sounded like a wind-up bird I heard once as a child.

Then, as the devices started to pass us, their trajectory began to change. They were arcing towards us! I just had time to yell "Brace…!" to our baffled crew before they impacted.

Now, to say the next few moments felt like time was standing still will seem like I'm trying to describe this instant using modern Hollywood action film techniques. That is not the case.

Here is what happened: three of the missiles hit the side of the ship, while the fourth missed. It was on a trajectory between our deck and our airbag. At the exact moment the missiles impacted there was a burst of pink smoke from the side of our ship, the exact color that the Chrononautilus filled with when they made the time jump. This cloud spread at an unrealistic speed across the deck, and whatever it hit froze in midair. Men snapped to a halt mid-leap, swinging ropes and lanterns locked at unnatural angles, the fourth missile stopped in the air in front of me, and I myself froze mid-stride.

After the initial shock of being frozen passed, I was given time to really study my unchanging view. The second of the four missiles seemed to have punctured one of the glass orbs of our Chrononautilus device. The pink gas inside it seemed to change the temporal state of whatever it touched.

Directly ahead of me, I could see the fourth mechanical projectile that had been fired at us. It looked like an aerodynamic shark fin made with a brass frame holding aluminum panels, mounted with lots of rivets. It was weighted at the bottom to keep it upright, and there was both a rear propeller to propel it forward as well as a front-sideways propeller, which would kick in mid-flight to alter its heading in that arching course that so successfully hit us. This device must have been made solely for the purpose of airship-to-airship aerial combat. An airship (just like a sea ship) is a fairly small target if you are aiming at the front of it. But being tall and long, a wide arcing shot would have a lot greater change of hitting. Provided you knew your distances and are skilled at timing the curve.

After what seemed like a long time (but was more likely just seconds) the pink gas started to disperse and turn into black fog. All the crew slowly regained motion. In fact, almost before my feet hit the deck the skies around us were filled with dark clouds. The missile that had been held midair in front of me slowly spun back to life, and whistled past and out of view.

My crew found footing and stood for a second, struggling to remember what was happening. Lightning from the newly formed clouds cracked and struck our ship, setting three ropes on fire. That woke me up, and I turned back to the wheel.

While time had frozen for us, the other airship had come about, and now their broadsides were pointed at us. Again, I heard the repeated *POOM!* of their cannons firing, and I pushed hard on the Elevator Wheel, in an attempt to lose altitude and dodge the shots.

The ship began to drop, but too slowly. Some of their shot hit the deck, some hit our sides, some our gasbag, puncturing it. This last hit would have been a huge problem for the *Hindenburg*, but *Ophelia's* airbag was not only filled with non-flammable gas, it was also sewn in an internal honeycomb pattern (we made these changes in the Black Forest redesign). A few holes would not affect buoyancy very much.

"Daniel, take the helm!" I yelled, and leaped down the stairs towards the grappling mounts. Our grappling gunners stood by as we needed them. "Target the gypsy wagon, and FIRE!"

These guys were good! Both gunners hit their mark, and were now reeling in the cargo. Soon it hung at an angle between the two airships, and at about this time our guns returned fire.

As the cannon fire rang painfully in my ears, I did the stupidest and most impressive thing in my life to date. I unbuckled the sword that I wore on a massive belt over one shoulder, and looped it around the grappling tether. Then I put one arm through the loop, and pushed off from the railing. I slid downward like a zip-line tourist, and came to a perfect stop right on top of the haul as it dangled between the two airships, miles above the ground.

Above my perch on the dangling haul, the other airship was returning fire, and *Ophelia* was taking a severe beating. Pieces of shattered wood and glass were raining down underneath her. I drew my sword, and began sawing at the ropes that tethered the other airship to the haul. When I cut through the first one, everything lurched, and I was nearly tossed off. In fact, I easily would have been except for some reason I had never unhooked my arm and belt from the tether I slid down on.

As the first rope was cut, the haul lurched round, swung me off my feet and shook me like a rag doll.

Still, the plan seemed to be working, so I unhooked my belt, and ran to the other tether and re-hooked it. From here I could barely reach the last rope with my sword. Above me, it looks like Daniel, at the helm of the *Ophelia*, had decided to turn the *Ophelia's* aft toward the other ship, in an effort to minimize the size of the target. Either that or he figured that captain's quarters should take the majority of the damage, as a punishment for my bad decisions today. At the same time he was dropping altitude to get under the enemy's guns, which would save lives in the short term but expose our airbag which could ultimately lead to our ruin.

With each volley the other airship launched, I could see her cannons fire, then they would pull the guns back in to reload. In another few minutes the guns would be pushed back out their hatch, to fire again. There were maybe ten gun ports on the ship, and only two or three cannons would fire at any time, each doing a significant bit of damage. As I sawed at the ropes, I watched the cannons all stop and all retreat into the hull. In a few seconds, they all pushed back out again, all loaded for one simultaneous volley that would easily burst the side of the *Ophelia*.

This was going to end up like our mission in Germany. Or worse, and Doctor Calgori was not here to bail us out of this one.

I felt helpless and hopeless down on the haul. Again, I had led us on reckless heroics, and again they had ended in embarrassment and disaster. If we lived through this, I doubted I'd still be captain – my track record was not so great at this point. Our Chrononautilus was cracked, so we were trapped in this dangerous time we didn't understand. And soon our precious, beloved ship would be burst like a piñata, scattering crew and friends into the air six thousand feet above the plains.

Then they fired. Ten huge guns erupted at easy range to our gas bag, but at the same time the final tether holding the haul to the enemy airship snapped. The haul dropped and with its massive weight. It jerked the *Ophelia* down and out of range of the enemy's guns before their shot could reach us!

We plummeted, out of range of the enemy, back into the clouds. Our descent slowed after a thousand terrifying feet of brutal descent, and the ship started to turn on a new course and speed away as fast as she could. In clouds, the other ship would have a hard time finding us. We'd escaped with the cargo!

In a few hours, the *Ophelia* found the Neobedouin caravan. We lowered their haul down to them, and climbed down ourselves into the midday heat of the grassy plains.

"We are indebted to you, Skyway Man," said the old chieftain. "But your ship looks like it has seen better days." Over my shoulder he could see the shattered hull, and the Chrononautilus, cracked, clear and empty.

I, too, was the worse for wear. I was filthy, windblown, bleeding in a few spots, and so tired I could feel my arms shaking. "Yeah, we got your supplies back, but I'm not sure it was worth the price we paid." And then I realized the true price we just paid. "At this point, we won't be able to get back to my time. Not with the Chrononautilus broken."

"Can you not repair it?" he asked.

"No. The only man who could has...well, he was also a casualty of this journey. I'm afraid we can't go..." I said, beginning to feel a deep aching in my chest. There was something that hurt deep inside. I could feel it gnawing at the edge of my consciousness, trying to dig out of someplace deep and dark inside me. My thoughts drifted to my band that died the night we collided with the *Ophelia*. And then to Lilith Tess, and Doctor Calgori. I was getting sad, angry and confused as I struggled in my exhaustion to figure out how these people were all connected.

The chief was looking deeply at me while I fought back these thoughts, and he interrupted my thoughts with, "Then don't go there yet! It seems like you'll have to do some searching here, first." He raised his walking stick and pointing southwest he said, "Follow those coal-fire streaks in the sky, and you'll soon come to the city of High Tortuga. There you might find the trail of a man who can fix your airship."

HIGH TORTUGA

We didn't stay long, maybe another hour or two, as a few of the Neobedouin men asked to join our tiny ragtag band, and I discussed with their chieftain whether it would hurt their tribe.

Soon we were aloft, and following the coal-fire trails, black cloudy streaks like the vapor trails of commercial airliners. These were the coal-fire smoke of steam-powered airships, chugging like trains of old, headed to High Tortuga.

The heat of the plains warped our vision, rippling the air and confusing perspective. When I first saw the rickety old buildings of High Tortuga and the many swinging bridges between them, it was those ripples of hot air that I assumed explained their appearance of floating in the air. But as we got closer, I saw the true explanation was that a hundred massive balloons and a thousand or more ropes held this city, a floating island, two miles above the wasteland prairies.

There were dozens of styles of airships pulling up to the docks that circled the city. Airships of all sizes, from massive clusters of balloons with several buildings underneath to sleek sloops like ours, to small one-man units with propellers on back packs pulling cart-like baskets on their own balloons.

Standing near me at the wheel, Kristina asked, "I wonder why we don't see airplanes? I mean, there are more kinds of flying machines than I could have imagined, but no airplanes."

"No helicopters either," Tanner said.

"I'll bet it's about fuel costs. Keeping a plane indefinitely in the air doesn't sound cheap. These guys are doing whatever they can to stay above all those beasts below. They *live* up here!" said Daniel.

"Yeah, and I'll wager landing on those precarious planks isn't something you'd want to do in a biplane," I added, wary of the coming challenge of making this huge ship stop next to the docks without grinding into them or any of the other airships. "Even if a dock was long enough to work as a runway, you still have all the ropes holding things up. They could take off your wings. That just sounds like a bad time."

The docks were crowded with men, women and children, tying ropes, unloading cargo, and selling birds and beasts like fish on a wharf. There were huge machines attached to gas tanks that filled the airbags of the airships, and small wooden cranes hoisting cargo in and out of the them.

We steered confidently in. Or say, I did my best to give the appearance of confidence as we headed towards one of the docks. Men came out and stood at the ready by yard-long mooring cleats, so we threw them ropes. Soon a gangplank was extended, and I walked down it to meet with a red-faced, barrel-chested smiling man, who said, "Aye, she's a 'beaut! That's the best replica I've ever seen!" He was looking at our ship. "She looks just like the pictures of the *Ophelia* in the old newspapers from the ruins. In fact, other than that shattered hull, I'd say it was the actual *Ophelia*. Oh, and shouldn't there be a big glass orb right in the middle there? Even still, you guys must really love your history!"

I said nothing, and we set off down the sun-bleached wood of the streets of High Tortuga. The outer docks were a bustle of commotion, but once inside their rings, the streets were peaceful and sunny, with only occasional shadows from the massive balloons that held the city from far above.

There were birds everywhere, and many of the railings were covered with their filth. Small children chased them, fed them, or caught them in large nets to take home for the supper pots.

The people of High Tortuga were a mismatched bunch. All

skin colors, from fair and pink, sunburned and freckled, to black as pitch and covered in copper tattoos. There were huge tricorn hats and helmets as well as all hair types–braided beards and colored Mohawks, and curly blond ringlets so fair they looked like they were made of clouds. Some of the people wore huge coats, boots, and belts with swords or pistols in them. While others wore very little; vests, short pants and sunburned skin. Most had goggles on their eyes or foreheads, since there was often a strong wind blowing, making it hard to see.

The buildings were not tall, one or two stories mostly. They were hand built of wood, mostly unpainted on the outer rings, but more ornate towards the center of the city, which appeared to be the location of the most favored homes.

We followed some signs, written in what looked like a stylized but readable variety of English, towards a pub called "The Weary Banshee". Honestly, I'm not really sure why we were headed there, other than we were tired, and I hadn't set foot in a pub in ages. It sounded like bliss.

We found the pub in a teetering building, hanging lower than the rest of the city. A porch and portholes that ran around the bottom floor had a three hundred and sixty degree view of the grasslands and hills below High Tortuga.

We walked down a steep swinging bridge that led to a pair of doors, not the swinging saloon doors of the Old West I expected, but two heavy oak doors, with a big sign saying "Pull hard". This we did, and in fact it took two of us to pull the massive creaking doors open, and we then stepped into a truly foreign place.

The first thing that struck us was the appearance that there was no floor! That wasn't the case. The floor was completely made of thick glass, so the occupants could see what was going on under the city. Small, sturdy round aluminum tables were placed around the glass floor, with all manner of shadowy characters silhouetted against the sky beneath them. There were no candles or fires of any kind. Only a single large brass stove that sat in the corner of the room, with pipes and fans to push heat out. On the walls hung huge propellers, drawn swords, and framed sepia pictures of old airships, including...

"Oh, man, look at this!" Daniel pointed to a picture of a familiar craft. "That's the *Ophelia*!" He was pointing to a news clipping that had been framed, that told of our exploits in the 1920s over the jungles of the Amazon Delta.

"Oh, what the hell!" Tanner said.

"Shush!" Daniel interrupted. "Keep your voice down." He had moved onto the next framed news article. "If I'm understanding this correctly, it looks like we have not exactly been going about our missions undetected! We'd jump to the next destination, while people were writing articles about us! These guys see us as Santa Claus, or some team of super-heroes or something! Popping up through time to solve some world problem."

Awesome, I thought. We're superheroes!

Kristina rolled her eyes. "Thank god we didn't stop to sign autographs! We're lucky they don't have pictures of us any closer then this," she said, pointing to a distant shot of the *Ophelia* over a mosque in Istanbul. "If they did, I don't think we'd have been able to get through the crowds at the docks!"

"Yeah, and I'll bet they're not happy with us." Tanner said. "We've been missing for two hundred years, and the world has gotten pretty messed up."

"It's gotten pretty damn cool, too," I said.

At this point a short, stout man in a silk coat and paisley top hat drew everyone's attention toward the center of the room. "Ladies and Gentleman." And then he laughed. "Who am I kidding, we got neither here." The room chuckled and he began again, "Scoundrels and pirates, turn your attention to the stage!"

The man made a exaggerated gesture to a small platform in the center of the room, little bigger than a coffee table, with a small round lump in the middle of it, "I present to you a delicate treat of petite proportions!" At this the lump unwound itself, and stood up. A delicate ballerina of eighteen gracefully lifted her arms over her head in an arch. She wore a translucent tutu, and pointe shoes, but it was clear that no other clothing was visible in the under light from the windows below.

"This *finely* crafted treasure. Nay, this Porcelain goddess of tender age and beauty, has been built purely for your pleasure!" Somewhere in the room a steam-powered calliope started puffing out a gentle waltz, in tones that reminded me of circus music.

The girl lifted herself to her toes, then slowly and without falter, lifted one leg up into the air and she hugged it. With a small twist she began to spin slowly on the other toe, as the narrator said, "She was crafted deep inside the cages of Desolation, from which her maker will never emerge! Yes, his cunning skill is obviously a genius the cities can't endure, just as her skin has a smoothness that even silk can't rival!"

As she spun, she extended one delicate arm, and when her back was turned towards us a large copper winding key could be seen extending from it. Her skin was a bit translucent on her back, and intricate gears could be seen spinning beneath as the key slowly turned.

Daniel gazed absentmindedly from a bar stool, and Tanner sat backward on a chair. Neither took their eyes off the doll for a moment. She stopped her slow spin, and stepped off the platform delicately *en pointe*, arms lifted above her head.

"Now gentlemen, or ladies, if the mood so strikes you," the man in the paisley hat continued. "This fine delicacy is not here merely for you to gawk at from a distance! Oh no, this is a dish you may enjoy alone, for a time..." He paused, and then added with a lecherous tone "...And for a significant price! Imagine if you will, while she gracefully floats across the floor now, imagine how she can slither and grind in your bed!"

"Oh, we need to get her alone!" It was Kristina who had spoken. If it was possible, Daniel and Tanner's jaws gaped a bit wider than they already were as they turned to face her.

"Um, we do?" I asked my wife with apprehension. I didn't know where she was going with this.

"Yes, we do!" she was whispering excitedly now. "Look at her, she's beautiful. She's graceful, she's amazing!"

I blushed. "Um, yes," I said, feeling like I was being lured into a trap but still willing to take the bait.

Kristina turned towards me, and her look changed to one of a patronizing big sister. "She is amazingly *well made*. Who ever made her obviously is a very skilled engineer and scientist. Whoever he is, he could possibly fix the Chrononautilus on the *Ophelia*! We need to get her alone to find out where her maker is!" Daniel and Tanner looked suddenly disappointed.

"Let's start the bidding at thirty-five!" said the small announcer, and a dozen hands went into the air. Kristina lifted her hand to bid, and the announcer chuckled. "Now that's a sight I'd like to see! Okay, boys, don't let this pretty lady bidder intimidate you! This is a dish you need to taste!"

In a few moments the auction was over. Kristina had won, and the small announcer put the ballerina's hand in hers. "Take your time, girls, but get her back to me before sun-up." And with this he gestured towards stairs that led to obviously seedy apartments. Kristina and the doll walked towards the steps, the doll gracefully on the tips of her toes the whole time. Just before she disappeared up the stairs, Kristina nodded for me to follow. I did, but I have to admit I felt a little tingly inside.

I walked as inconspicuously as I could up the stairs a few yards behind the girls, and as I reached the top I saw them disappear into a room together. I knocked at the door, and Kristina opened it abruptly and pulled me in.

The doll was in the center of the bed kneeling, her transparent pink tutu flared around her small legs, and as her eyes flicked off Kristina's to me, she said "Oh!" with surprise. Then she added, "Two is fine, but you have to be gentle with me. I break."

"Actually," Kristina said, "We have a question for you."

The doll looked suspicious, and her little hands balled up into fists. "Yes?"

Seeing the doll's apprehension, Kristina sat on the bed next to her. Speaking in a gentle tone she asked, "Do you mind terribly if we ask who made you?"

The doll *did* mind! She leaped to her feet, and grabbed a propeller shaped chandelier above us, and swung over Kristina. She would have swung right over me, and gone out the door, but mid swing the chandelier broke free, and crashed to the ground with her under it. She lay angrily pinned under it, her leg jutted out from under her body at an unnatural-looking angle.

"Whoa, whoa!" I said, and I stooped to help lift the chandelier off her, "What was that? Are we not allowed to ask you that?"

She tried to stand, but her broken leg would not support her. She started to cry tiny golden tears that flowed slowly down her porcelain-like cheeks. "What will you do with me?"

"What? Nothing!" I said. "What do you mean?"

"You are not peelers? You don't fill the Change Cage?" she asked, now looking as confused as I was.

"No, we don't! We don't even know what that is!" I said desperately.

"Look, we are not from around here, and we don't really know the rules," Kristina said. "We really don't wish to harm you at all, its just that we are in big trouble and we need someone who's good at building and fixing. I saw the gears through your back, and assumed whoever made you could help us." Kristina then added, "You look…complex."

"I am," the doll said, not giving a hint as to which meaning of the word she was acknowledging. But she relaxed, and I helped her up to the side of the bed. We all quietly looked at her leg. As I held it in my hands, I could feel it was not a "bone is broken" sort of break, but a "pistons and chains have pulled loose under the skin" sort of break. It rattled when I moved it. This is not something that would heal - it had to be fixed.

"I don't know who made me," she said, and she looked out the porthole window toward the sunset. From here we could see the grassy plains, the horizon, and the setting sun. Just above the horizon we could see a cluster of airships, all uniformly built with black gondolas and black ballonets. These were just visible under the docks and airships at the edge of the city. As this cluster of black airships drew closer, bells started ringing in the distance, and just as we heard them, the enclosing airships fired!

Torpedoes in the sky, self-propelled rockets whistled away from their hulls towards the docks. Their impact shook the city in waves, and cast its citizens off the bridges and into the sky. I could hear commotion in the bar below us, and I now knew why its patrons felt more comfortable dining while keeping their eyes on the horizon.

Another impact sent the room swinging, and the doll desperately grabbed my arm. "Take me with you. I am not allowed to be!"

"What?" I asked.

"Take me with you, and I will help you find my maker! My brother knows where he is, he can take you to him!" She held her arms out to me imploringly.

I glanced at Kristina, who nodded, so I picked up the doll and put her over one shoulder as delicately as I could, while saying, "Tell me if I hurt you." Like this the three of us ran from the room.

As we came down the stairs, Tanner and Daniel were coming up. "Hey, I think it's time to leave," Daniel said. Another explosion painted the sky red, and swung the Inn harshly.

"What gave you that idea?" I said as the five of us ran towards the door.

"Well, for starters, everyone else left," Daniel said. "Kind of in a hurry, too."

We ran up the ramp, and when we got to the streets we could see the docks were ablaze. Airships were starting their propellers, and the small black fleet was drawing closer, firing shot after shot into the port, clearing themselves a place to dock.

Many men and woman ran past us down the massive hanging bridge that led to our ship. They brandished a wide array of weapons, some obvious like swords or rifles, and some not so obvious. I saw one man rolling a device that looked like a wheelbarrow, with one wheel and two handles and triggers. On top was a series of brass orbs connected to two large cones that pointed out the front. "*Aetheric Condenser Cannon*" read a little plaque on the side. I might never know what it does, but I'm guessing you shouldn't stand in front of it!

Another torpedo hit the docks where our swinging bridge anchored to them. The shockwave rolled down the bridge like a wave on the ocean, and tossed the townspeople like rag dolls off a bedspread.

"Hold on!" I yelled, and we all grabbed the railings and prepared to be thrown. The doll tightened her small soft arms around me, just as the bridge lifted and tossed us into the air. For a moment, my feet were above me, and a second later we were back on our feet running.

The black fleet was now firing grappling lines into the dock, and pulling their ships up to port. A new problem was making itself clear. The *Ophelia* was at the end of the large pier ahead of us, and between it and ourselves the black ships were docking. Out of them came soldiers, uniformed in black leather, canvas pants, and tall black leather boots. Everything about them was shiny, proper and oppressive. They pulled polished chrome pistols from black leather holsters and shot men, women and children alike.

One of the soldiers had a megaphone, and he yelled into it in a matter-of-fact voice, "You have violated population control and confinement law, as set out by His Majesty Emperor Victor the First. Any person found outside the cities will be considered a traitor to the balance of nature, and will be executed, or fed to the fauna, at the convenience of the Imperial Navy." He read this as if he had read it every day of his life. No enthusiasm. He read it because it was his job, and everyone knew exactly what he was talking about.

"Wow, that is not right!" said Tanner, as he and Daniel drew swords.

We headed towards the *Ophelia*, trying to navigate through the frantic mob on the docks that was either running towards, or away from the naval soldiers. As we rounded a large stack of wooden shipping crates, we found ourselves face to face with a squad of six black-uniformed men with rifles. The squad leader looked at the doll on my shoulder, and the key coming out of her back, and said, "Where are you taking this piece of obviously illegal horology?"

"Um, to you! I figured you'd wanted to see this!" I said, but he didn't buy it for a second.

"Gentlemen, aim!" he commanded, but as they hoisted their rifles to their shoulders, a shadow flashed over our heads. Between the soldiers and us, a young Neobedouin had leaped, and the dreadlocks coming out from under his headwrap dripped with blood. We had never seen this boy before, and he glanced past us to the doll on my shoulder. Then he lifted his arms, and each wrist was strapped to the handle of two double-bladed scythes.

"So you want to be first, beast dancer?" said the officer, "So be…" but the Neobedouin boy jumped up in a spin of whirling blades that slashed the throats of the officer and the two soldiers next to him.

He landed again, and leaped onto the shoulders of the soldier to his right as the soldier to his left fired at him, killing his comrade. The Beast Dancer then did a kind of a backward cartwheel, slicing open the bellies of the two remaining navy men.

The tribal boy then turned to us, and said to the doll, "I know you cannot love, but I will always love you!" and he rushed forward into the last remaining group of soldiers blocking us from our ship. As he cleared the path for us, I heard the doll whisper to herself, "But I can love."

We ran up the gangplank of the *Ophelia* as she was beginning to pull away from the docks. Jean-Paul looked at the clockwork girl on my back, and said casually, "Hey, where'd you get the doll?" He assumed she was just an inanimate thing, like a mannequin. The doll spun her head around to Jean-Paul and glared. "I am not owned!" she said, stunning the pirate. He stumbled backward into a spool of rope.

"It – she! Talks!" he stammered.

"And she's *complicated*," Kristina grumbled. "Watch what you say around her, or she'll break herself some more." Kristina rolled her eyes.

I propped the doll up against the mast as the acting-pilot was pulling the ship away from the dock. He pulled hard on the elevator wheel, spinning frantically to drop the ship's altitude below the firing line of the assaulting airships of the Imperial Navy.

"Okay, so it would appear there *is* a government in this time, and they are not particularly freedom-loving," Daniel said. "What do you think he meant by 'population control' and 'confinement law'?"

"The Neobedouin chief told me about this," I said.

"People are not allowed to live outside the Cities," the doll said, sensing our confusion. "The Victorians – that is, Emperor Victor's supporters – are kept in huge walled cities. It's supposed to be for the sake of the *environment*, and the *balance of nature*. Victor says humans spread like a disease, and if left to breed uncontrolled they would soon destroy the planet with their sheer numbers."

The doll continued, "So he keeps them locked up. He also keeps them from advancing technologically so he can keep them powerless to rebel against him. 'Evolution Instigates Manifest Destiny' he says, meaning that if man evolves they will expand in numbers until they've covered the world.

"My kind, Automatons, are also controlled. We are not allowed to be more advanced than basic machines with basic functions. Otherwise we are considered 'evolution', and will be disassembled. But some of our makers started making us very complex, and we became aware. In the cities, Automatons must hide this part of themselves; they must pretend to be simple machines. But a few of us escape."

"So wait, why were those ships attacking the city?" I asked.

"That entire city is illegal. The Emperor does not sanction it. There are a few floating cities and skylands that have sprung up out here in the free world. The Navy attacks them, and often burns them down. They won't get High Tortuga, though. It's too heavily defended. This is just a stunt to let the free people know they are still considered illegal. Most of those people have either escaped from the cities, or were illegally born. If caught alive, they will be fed to the wild predators, or at least that's what used to happen back in the time of the first world Emperor. It doesn't happen much anymore, since they rarely catch people alive. The Imperial Navy is not big enough to take on all the

Airship Pirates, as they call any of the sky peoples. While the Emperor is keeping populations down with his people, the free peoples are breeding and growing in number to the point where he can no longer find them all. So he attacks from time to time, just to keep things in balance."

We were quiet for a while considering this, and then I said, "Well, if you are going to be traveling with us, we should know your name."

"My name is Timony," she said. "My brother is Gyrod. He is the one you will need if you need to find father. He worked for a family in the city of Everglade. The family he protects escaped the city, and now lives in the bayou in a home he built them."

She paused for a moment. "He does not know I have left the city. I've been trying to get to him, but no sky people will take me to him. Honestly, we haven't seen each other since the shop days. I was bought by a theater producer, and since then we have only passed notes back and forth to each other."

"And you think he can help us?" I asked.

"Yes. He helped his family escape with the help of our father – our maker. But our father was thrown into the Cage when the Victorians found out. My brother suffers from the guilt of this, and has sworn to go back and free our father."

"How do we find your brother?" Daniel asked.

"That will be tricky. His family lives in the swamps around Everglade. It's many miles from the city, so their home and farm cannot be seen from the city towers, but your airship would be spotted easily. You'll have to find another way to get there."

As she said this, I found I was sitting on the front tire of

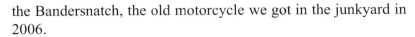

the Bandersnatch, the old motorcycle we got in the junkyard in 2006.

"I think I know how to reach him," I said.

Automaton

Hundreds miles from the city of Everglade, in an early morning haze, we lowered my motorcycle to the ground. It finally stopped swinging when it touched the dust of the deserted highway that was once the southeast of Texas.

In the sidecar I stowed a shotgun and shells, cans of chili that could have been eighty years old or more (I dared not guess what I would find on opening these), a bedroll in case my trip took more then a couple days, a canteen of water, and a half bottle of rum…in case I needed pain killer for reasons yet unrevealed. The drive would be at least ten hours. If I could make it in that amount of time on a bike this old, I would be very sore in some very delicate places.

After I climbed down the rope ladder to the ground, the *Ophelia's* engines growled angrily, and she slipped away west where she would wait as far from any known Imperial cities or outposts as she could.

There is a bizarre ritual to starting a Chang Jiang motorcycle. I doubt any are still alive who understand the reasons behind it. I only hoped I would remember it. First, turn the fuel on. Tap the carburetor, and check the fuel gauge to make sure gas is pouring in, double-check that you are in neutral; roll the engine over by stepping down on the kickstart. This is to make sure it's getting fuel all throughout the engine. Turn the switch on, advance the throttle a smidge. Then jump on the kick-starter at least ten times, and hope she comes to life.

Here at the End of Days, in the middle of the wastelands, with my only friends and family five hundred feet up and rising in a world with no cell phones, I kicked once, twice…ten times… twenty times…

I must have flooded it. I aired it out and started over. I pulled the fuel cap to check the gas. I pulled the carburetor, to let the flooded gas evaporate. I thought to check if the fuel mixture was correct, and realized I would really have no idea how to tell if it was correct or not. In the end it took more then forty kicks, but it finally started.

A pistol in my face could hardly have scared me more than that much isolation, mixed with that much desolation and no transportation! But once on the road, the first couple of hours were joyous! The wind blowing through my hair, road under my wheels. A sunny day, and no helmet laws!

There were cacti, and tumbleweeds. There were rocky hills and sweeping valleys. There were bushy little clusters of trees surrounding little lakes, pretty as any oasis you may have imagined reading *1001 Arabian Nights*. Tiny little animals darted across the road constantly; small birds, lizards, jackrabbits, armadillo, and a few things I didn't recognize.

I passed many "ruins" as the Neobedouins referred to them. Empty houses, a hundred years abandoned and overgrown with long-dead vines. Cars, rusted to the point that if I stood on them with one foot, I would go right through. I saw massive skeletons of rust that had once been skyscrapers. Ghost town after ghost town, consumed by sand or trees.

It was a world of flotsam and jetsam being slowly swallowed by nature. The ruined empires of days gone by.

I passed a Neobedouin Caravan that was headed in the other direction. I smiled and waved. They looked at me as if I was insane - insane for traveling the wastelands alone, I'll wager, yet the full rationale for this was yet to be revealed to me.

Interestingly, these guys weren't using semi-cabs to pull their caravan, but massive beasts. The creatures weren't exactly dinosaurs, they were mammals, but they were easily three times the size of an elephant. They had bodies with about the proportions of an elephant, yet much larger, with long necks and small heads. They were slow and lumbering, but strong and friendly. They were also a little timid in nature, and they leaned away from my bike as I rumbled past.

I can only assume these were beasts the Emperor's predecessor had brought back from extinction in an effort to "restore balance". If so, why bring these creatures back? Was it to have a large enough food source to feed the now teaming populations of man-eating predators?

Each massive beast pulled one or two multi-floored hauls as the tribe rode around them on camels. I could hardly imagine a more exotic scene than the pale yellow sands, the brightly painted hauls, the turbaned riders, and the strange assortment of beasts from large to immense!

That was not the only unusual wildlife I saw. I almost lost my life that evening to a herd of deer-sized beasts with antlers like a gazelle, and what appeared to be two short trunks! I have no idea what they were, but they were spread thickly on the road in a massive herd of at least a hundred beasts. I had just crested a small hill and when I cleared the top I found myself plunging into the herd. They only just darted to the side in time to allow me to break right inyo the middle of the herd.

I sat, engine rumbling and sputtering, in the middle of this mass of stupid and timid animals. As the sun started to set, I honked my little horn to try to get them to move. They just plodded slowly onward, hardly noticing me and at times even bumping into me. I must have sat there a good twenty minutes, wondering what to do, and thinking of the shotgun.

In my head I had started to call them elelope. That's "elephant" plus "antelope", since they looked like an antelope with a couple small elephant trunks. "Antephant' really didn't seem to fit them. Eventually something spooked them. The beasts at the head of the herd started to turn back around, making a panicked noise that sounded desperate and fearful. The dumb beasts around me did nothing to alter their course, and some were knocked down as the others pushed in.

Finally, the entire herd started to run in the other direction, and I could see why. When I looked back over their heads, I could see three beasts as large as SUVs, hunched and spread in a stalking formation. They had thick prickly fur, long at the shoulders, but short on their legs and hindquarters, and a spotted pattern like hyenas. Their immense size would have made a Siberian tiger cower and run. I swear I could *smell* them coming.

I couldn't really move until the herd had raced past, but when I could I gunned the engine, and darted to one side. This sound, however, drew the beasts' attention. The nearest leaped a good twenty feet toward me. I saw him coming, and I turned to the side, throttling hard. When he landed where I had been, he slid six feet in the dirt and gravel. A drawback of being that large is that you have more inertia, so stopping isn't easy. A house cat would have changed directions instantly upon hitting the ground, and would have pinned me before I could get away. By the time he corrected his course, I was now bulleting full speed through the herd.

It leaped again, but I was not so much his target anymore, as he was interested in catching the nearest prey. It pinned some poor beast behind me and stood on it as it thrashed briefly, and then succumbed to its fate.

This I saw through my rearview mirror. I didn't turn my head to look back.

In a few moments, I burst out the front of the herd and

headed down the empty road with a new fear and respect for the growing darkness around me.

Over the next few hours, the sides of the road began to fill with trees, and I crossed over many little bridges, until finally I was on a raised spit between long, low marshes. Fireflies swirled in the bushes, and the sounds of croaking frogs could be heard audibly over the engines.

Finally, the road turned to wooden planks. This dock and its skewed pylons led about a quarter mile out to a small shack. The sky had turned to midnight blue, dark and foreboding between the trees, but there was a warm inviting glow coming from the shack. Silhouetted in this light was a large crouched figure, seven feet tall, with unnaturally square shoulders.

He held in his hand what looked like a demolition bar–a six-foot long steel bar that is used to tear apart buildings or cars. It's nearly as thick as your wrist, and is immensely heavy. The shadow held it lightly in one hand, and a dim glow came from where its eyes must be.

"Turn away, Bedouin. Your tribe is elsewhere. *My* road ends here," said the voice, raspy, yet strong and threatening. It spoke with the confidence of a man who had won a hundred confrontations of this nature, but this was not a man.

I got off my bike.

"Turn back, Bedouin. Your motion will bring the crocs. They know I am not their food, so they leave me alone, but I'm sure they can smell you already." At this, something moved in the water.

My eyes searched the black marsh, and I swear I saw a beast the size of a school bus slowly shift under the blackness to point towards me.

"Gyrod, I'm here to speak to you. Your sister has sent me! She has left the city, and wants to see you!" I yelled back to him.

Two things happened at once. First, a massive exaggeration of a crocodile, thirty feet long, with crooked teeth the size of my feet, eyes wild and hungry, put one massive clawed foot onto the dock. Its head and body lay under the water nearly out of view, and it lifted the tip of its nose into the light and snorted.

The other thing that happened was that a small child of five, in a little white lacy dress, slipped past her stoic guardian, and was running towards me unaware of the beast in the water!

The Automaton yelled in a voice of pained fear and pity, "This is not your father, Isabella, come back to the house!"

The child was nearly to where the beast lay in wait, her eyes on me, and I could see the lizard's huge nostrils flair as it took in her scent. It was slowly raising its mouth from the water in perfect anticipation.

I didn't think. Forgetting my shotgun, I leaped from my bike and ran toward her. At the same time, the clockwork man started toward the beast, but as he took his second step, a rattling, scraping sound came from his torso, a kind of *Screeeee-chika-chika-chika-chika*! He grabbed at his chest in pain. This sound drew the attention of the beast, and as it swung its head up over the dock to look, the weight of its massive claw broke through, knocking the child to the ground.

I ran to her, and fell on the uneven dock. Together we slid towards the beast, and as my boots hit it, I grabbed the child. The beast swung its head back around and over us, and it opened its foul, blackened mouth.

At this point, the clockwork man pounded his chest hard, denting the metal, which made the scraping sound quiet, then he leaped into the air. The wrecking bar came down on the head of the beast, and in doing so changed the shape of its skull. At this the beast thrashed in the water and its tail swung into the dock sending planks spinning into the air.

The automaton pulled the bar back, and thrust it into the beast's cheek. The bar sank two feet into the dark green flesh, and the beast pulled back from the dock in horror, swinging the man like a rag doll.

I held the child, stood, and ran for the house. As I ran, I watched the clockwork man standing astride the beast. He lifted the bar again to strike, but as he did the rattling scraping sound came again. *Screeeee-chika-chika-chika –chika!*. He froze mid-swing and stumbled backward into the water.

The beast pulled back, facing where the clockwork man had sunk, and slowly submerged.

I ran up the porch of the house, stumbling on an overturned dollhouse, and threw open the screen door. I set the child on a wooden bench, and with a "Stay!" I turned and ran back out.

On the porch stood the automaton, with scraped and stained copper and brass fittings dripping with mud, black blood, and swamp grass. He grasped at his chest in pain.

All he said was, "My sister?"

FATHER

The cabin was a single room, containing a small dinette set, a kitchen, a double bed, and two child-sized beds. We put five-year-old Isabella in a bed next to her eight-year-old sister who had managed to sleep through the night's events.

The little cabin was a mess. Dishes were on the floor with half-eaten food stuck to them. Spoons and plates stuck to the blankets of the beds. Couch cushions had been taken from the old sofa, and arranged into a fort in the center of the room. There was a pile of unopened canned food in the corner of the kitchen, and a pile of old half-emptied cans on the floor around it.

"I apologize for the mess," said the brass man. "But I have been traveling further and further away to find food for them. The girls are good, and stay inside when told, but they do make a mess when I'm gone."

Visibly tired, he began to tidy up. "I was not made for domestic duties," he said, trying his best to pick up a glass bowl with his huge brass fists. "I was not made to take care of children. I was made to protect, not to nurture. But with their parents dead six months now, 'protecting' has more responsibilities than it used to."

He was quiet for a minute. "Tell me of my sister."

So I told him of the doll, and the floating city. I told him of our airship, and the broken Chrononautilus.

"I guess our ship needs some work. How about you? What is that grating sound I keep hearing whenever you are about to do something strenuous?" I said.

"My flywheel. I have weighted wheels inside me. When I am about to leap or run, or swing my rod, it spins up inertia that I can then use for extra momentum. But it's been damaged. Bent. It doesn't fit just right any longer, and so as it spins it vibrates and drags against my heart. This heats up, and can occasionally lock things up inside until I cool," he said.

"Can it be replaced?" I asked.

"I don't know. I found a replacement, in a...well, a few miles from here. But I don't know what will happen it I take the old one out. I could die," he said.

"Forgive my ignorance, but couldn't you just be restarted? Perhaps if I..." I said, but he interrupted me.

"It doesn't work like that," he said.

We had talked now so long the sun was beginning to rise. As it did the children woke.

First the eldest woke up, and she sat in bed staring at me with her blinking, sleep-blurred eyes. She was a girl of eight, with red pigtails and a freckly face. Her eyes were green, and looked like they had seen recent tears. As she watched me, she absentmindedly took a small, broken plastic crown from her night stand and put it on her head, as if it was simply what one did first thing in the morning.

When the other child woke, without opening her eyes she got out of her bed and climbed into her sister's, and hugged her. Then, still without opening her eyes she went back to her bed, grabbed a rag doll from under her pillow, and then got back into bed with her sister.

Gyrod said, "Eventually the wheel is just going to freeze up. At that point I will stop. There is no way of telling when it will happen, but I will die."

Under his rasping deep tones, I heard a soft voice ask her sister, "Is that daddy?" They were looking at me.

"So I suppose I should just try to change the gear. But if I fail, the girls will be alone. And if I die because I didn't try to replace it, the girls will also be alone. "

Finally, the littlest one slipped out of her sister's lap, and crawled into mine. She pressed her small curly blond head (which smelled like a hug) against my chest and asked, "Daddy?"

I hugged her back, and said, "Sure."

Would you have done any different? It wasn't just Doctor Calgori's dying words to me. These tiny children had lost their father and mother when they were too young to remember them. They were barely taken care of by a dying guardian made of metal, who at any point could seize up and never move again. Then they would be alone, in a wasteland of man-eating beasts. No, don't kid yourself, you would have done the same damn thing. Even if you think yourself cruel enough to correct this babe with glistening eyes, "No, kid, I ain't your dad." But you are wrong. You'd have done the same thing.

I took a nap that morning, while the girls gleefully packed tiny suitcases full of things like crayons, dollhouse furniture, and other tiny toys their guardian had carefully plucked from the ruins with his massive metal hands. I never mentioned we were leaving, they just assumed.

When I woke, they excitedly asked me where we were going. "I guess we are going to live in the skies," I said. "Have you ever seen an airship?" They screeched with joy. This was too much– Daddy had returned after so long that they could no longer remember what he looked like, only to take them to the clouds to spend the rest of their life as angels!

"Or mermaids!" said Isabella.

"No, mermaids are in the water," Chloe said in the

condescending tones of a big sister.

"No, only monsters live in the water," Isabella said, with a dark and defiant look. Then she brightened. "We can be sky mermaids! Right, Daddy?"

"Uh, sure!" I said.

It was a hot, sticky day, and we took small suitcases outside, and strapped them onto the back of the bike. Then I loaded both girls into the sidecar, strapped the single seatbelt across their laps. They looked like they were about to go on their first roller coaster ride: excited, nervous and joyful. I went through the Bandersnatch's starting ritual, as little Isabella watched every step with absolute fascination. Chloe was straightening the blanket over their laps, and lining up their little dolls at their feet on the floor of the sidecar.

The brass man stood looking down at me. "I trust you to be their guardian. I have heard your stories, and I trust you can keep them safe. I will get my new flywheel, and meet you at the crossroads in three days time if I am still moving. Then we will go to my father together."

"I'll keep them safe, Gyrod. I might not be made of brass, but I've lived through a few things myself." I glanced at the girls, who looked up at me, doe-eyed. "I will keep them safe," I said, and with that I throttled back and rumbled down the dock and back down the bayou road.

> *Little Girl, in your dress of snowy white,*
> *Get behind me, safe from creatures of the night.*
> *With these arms and with these fists,*
> *I'll keep you safe and sound.*
> *Through the forests and the mists,*

We'll go down,

This dark and twisty road.

~ Excerpt from This Dark and Twisty Road

It was late in the morning when we started out, and we spent the better part of the day watching the trees and marshes of the bayou become more sparse, until finally as the sun started to set we broke through the last line of trees and back out onto the prairie.

The crickets, or cicadas, or whatever bug it is that sings at night, were so ferociously loud I could hear them over the small bike's sputtering engine. Chloe, the oldest girl, was now asleep. Her eyes where tightly shut under her small goggles and her red pigtails were waving in the wind. Isabella, the tiny girl in the white lace dress, was nearly to the land of Nod, but under her heavy eyelids she watched the sun stain the sky and distant mountains crimson.

I've got three wheels, and a frame of rust.

Blue skies above, and behind me dust.

Half a tank of gas won't get very far,

But you're safe from apocalypse, in Daddy's sidecar.

- Lyrics from "To the Apocalypse in Daddy's Side Car"

Honestly, I would have camped out at sunset myself. Laid my bedroll down and slept by my bike like a cowboy sleeps near his horse, except for the fear. I was afraid to stop moving for fear of what would catch me if I did. Earlier in the day, the girls pointed out several large beasts feasting on a dead thing. Their fresh kill rendered us completely uninteresting, but I was haunted by the thought that we would eventually meet hungry versions of these beasts.

Finally, just before dawn, I determined that the danger of falling asleep on my handlebars was just as life-threatening as being eaten in our sleep, so I pulled the bike off the side of the road into a cluster of trees, laid on a patch of dried grass, and fell instantly asleep.

Some hours later, I found myself struggling to keep my eyelids covered enough to sleep, while the harsh hot sun slow-roasted my skin. I rolled over, threw my arms across my head, then threw my coat over my head, which was way too hot, and finally remembered where I was, and the fact that we were out in the open. I pulled myself awake.

I sat urgently up, and gazed blearily around waiting for my eyes to get used to being opened. "Kids?"

I heard a tiny, "Yes, Daddy?"

"Where are you?" I asked, standing.

"Look! Sand castles!" I heard a pair of small voices say.

The girls were crouched on a little sandy beach by a small lake. Around the lake were various hot-climate trees including a few palms and a cactus or two. It was a perfect little desert oasis, and it looked like I had slept late into the morning while the girls had woken early and made palace after palace in the sand. From somewhere in the sidecar they had produced a pair of toy princesses, who now stood on top of their sandcastles.

The two were so engrossed with their peaceful play, that I couldn't bring myself to force them back on the road immediately, so I dug into the trunk (there was a little trunk area behind the seat in the side car) and pulled out the only food I had brought with me; canned chili. Upon pulling out the can, I realized I had not brought a can opener, but I had a big bowie knife, so I put the can on a large rock, put my boot on the can, and attempted to saw the top off with the knife.

"Daddy, what are you doing?" asked little five-year-old Isabella. Still calling me Daddy...that was going to take a bit of getting used to. Honestly, though, I must have been built for this job, since I found I wasn't even formulating a plan to pawn them off somewhere else. In a different era, I would have had to 'take them to the authorities', whatever that meant, and would never have seen them again. But this was not a time to pawn your troubles and responsibilities off on the system. This was a time to step up, and do things your damn self.

"Making breakfast," I said, while still struggling with the knife.

"We had oranges for breakfast. They were on the trees!" said Isabella.

"Would you like an orange?" asked Chloe, holding three freshly picked oranges in the upturned front of her skirt. I guess these little urchins were self-sufficient.

So we shared a few more oranges, then I buckled the kids back into the sidecar, and were off. I never did get that can of chili open.

We were crossing back over the open plain again. Hundreds of miles of pale yellow grass, unendingly speckled with little dry bushes. In the blue distance were mesas, and occasionally an airship could be spied far overhead, heading off on business I could not guess.

We passed more elelopes,or whatever they were, lumbering along with that same look of mildly nervous placidity. The girls were thrilled with these, excitedly pointing and yelling to each other over the wind and road noise.

Half of the massive mesas were crested with small towns. These only seemed accessible by air travel, much to our frustration. The girls were getting hungry, and the chili would require a longer stop then I wanted to make, so I'm afraid we spent the larger part of the day trying to find road access to one of the mesa-top towns. The irony that I spent half the day trying to get to a town so we wouldn't have to stop to make camp, which would have taken less time, was not lost on me. But now the sky was turning blood-orange, and the kids were looking exhausted and hungry.

Finally, after I was about to give up on finding town access and was starting to settle on the idea of stopping and making a fire to heat the damn chili (which I'm sure these little girls would have not enjoyed) we stumbled upon a beautiful little temporary city of tents. They were all colors of the rainbow in deep dry jewel tones, with tassels, golden ropes, flags and pikes. This mobile town lined both sides of the road with carts, shops, food stands and hauls.

There were dogs, too. One or two or three per tent. Beautiful, well-cared-for beasts, and only of the largest species. Great Danes, and Dobermans, and Mastiffs all stood watch over their family's homes. Although clean and well-fed, these were working beasts. They carried loads when the town was on the move, and they fought for their families' defense if beasts attacked. Many had deep scars, or were missing ears, but all were loved and respected.

This town was not just one Neobedouin tribe, but many, and the colors of each tribe could be plainly seen on the tents and flags of each triangular block. These torch-lit blocks all pointed toward a center square where a huge bonfire was blazing. As such, the bazaar/town formed a sort of spoked wheel, with every road leading towards the center.

Our little bike sputtered straight toward the crowded plaza without attracting any undue attention, and we came to a stop in front of a cluster of oil drum fires, on one of which skewered meat was cooking. I lifted the girls out of the sidecar, and hand-in-hand we walked to pick out our dinner from the friendly looking cart vendors.

All ages wandered the square, from bent old men to tiny children holding their parents' hands. They shopped, ate, played, and rested from the heat and labor of the day.

While we quietly ate in the growing blue shadows of the surrounding tents, musicians began to tune and play, while dancers stretched and strapped on their shoes and bracers around the fire. The music was the energetic blend of musical styles that I had heard from the Neobedouins before: Middle Eastern dance music, American blue grass, and Eastern European gypsy folk. This music was infectious, and it was starting to affect my little girls, just as it affected all the young around us. Their feet twitched, and they rolled around on their bottoms. I often had to remind Isabella to sit back down and finish eating this long-sought food – she kept standing to dance.

Finally, as the sky was starting to settle into deep purples and midnight blues, the dancers began. They circled the fire like children circle a maypole, weaving in and out. At the same time, they spun flaming balls on short ropes, and the musicians played their fiddles, darbukas, banjos and massive kettle drums. Then the circle broke into numerous sets of square-dancers, and they locked arms and spun, while swinging fire with their outside hands.

I was just taking notice of a dog barking and jumping at

something unseen away to the north of the town center when we were approached. A girl of eighteen, as brown as terra-cotta, with white-blonde dreadlocks and skin laced with fresh peeling henna, approached pig-tailed Chloe with a gentle smile. She handed the girls lit sparklers, took their hands and danced with them, teaching them how to spin arm in arm like the square dancers, and how to break and spin like a dervish when the music called for it.

I watched the kids in amazement: after an exhausting, grueling day's journey with nearly no food, all they needed was music and a bit of inspiration to be on their feet and spinning hand-in-hand like a carousel. I remember the thought flickering through my sleepy mind, *I wonder if young kids love to dance because it subconsciously reminds them of spinning in their mother's wombs. The beat of the drums matching the beat of their mother's heart, they themselves spinning like they spun inside the amniotic fluid.* I sketched some lyrics in my tiny note book:

> *Dance child, dance. Dance child, dance.*
>
> *Daylight is waning.*
>
> *Night times refraining.*
>
> *So dance my child.*
>
> *Dance, dance, my Isabella.*
>
> *Safely, in your carousella.*
>
> *Dance through the spinning,*
>
> *Just like your beginning.*
>
> *Dance, my child.*
>
> *Dance, my child.*
>
> *~ Excerpt from the song Sleep Isabella*

Then a young man ran through the center of the square with a panicked look on his face, waving his arms to try to get everyone's attention. When he reached the musicians, they stopped playing, and in the absence of the huge drum beats we heard it: the dogs were all viciously barking!

Immediately the whole town was in motion, running to their tents, and vehicles; swinging onto horses, kicking motorcycles to life, jumping onto the sides of dune-buggies. The dogs were let loose as the families took down their tents, and the beasts all ran to the northern edge of the town and stood in a pack barking into the darkness. I grabbed Chloe by the hand, and took Isabella under my arm and ran back to our Bandersnatch. They were scared, eyes wide and tearful. It didn't help that they were utterly exhausted. Placing the girls in the sidecar, I half-turned the ignition key to check the fuel. *Shit!* Less than a quarter tank. This was going to mean trouble.

I looked to the northern edge of the town, where the dogs were barking, and could see a growing cloud of dust was building in size and moving closer. I began the bike's starting ritual; prime carb, turn throttle once, kick, wait, et cetera. As I did this, I could see what was happening past the dogs. Low-flying airships were stampeding beasts towards us. What kind of creature didn't matter much, as there were thousands of them, and anything cow-sized or larger would trample this town flat. From what I had seen, there were lots of different beasts in the prairies big enough to crush this town to dust. Carnivores would strip the place clean like meat from a bone.

Scarred men and women in their twenties and thirties were strapping long split blades to their forearms. These were the "beast dancers", and they trained since birth to fight hand-to-hand with the likes of tigers and wolves, and hyenadon. They stood stoically in the midst of the pack of dogs, while the less combat-capable nomads threw the last of their camps onto their hauls and started heading south.

Seeing this heroic last-stand, I felt the familiar tightening of my chest, and steeling of my resolve. I pulled my shot gun from the holster that held it to my front fork, and turned the bike toward the oncoming stampede. I gunned the throttle, and the bike leapt forward, but this caused the girls to scream. Every foot towards the stampeding beasts increased their horror. I looked into the sidecar. They were terrified, clutching each other, wet wild eyes reflecting the fires and torches around us.

Here is where I realized something that had never occurred to me before. My heroic responsibility was no longer for "the town", or any strangers who needed saving. My responsibility was for these children. I was *their* hero, now, and no one else's. If I plunged into battle, and died, they would surely die. If I left them here, I would likely not find them again. If I took them into battle they would die. Heroics is not a game for parents. Or say, parents are heroes daily, but only for their kids; they can't be spared elsewhere.

So I spun the bike around and headed south with the rest of the caravan, while the warriors met the beasts head-on. I'm not sure how that ended for them, I was not around to see it.

REUNIONS

I decided it was best to drive all night, and being agitated as I was, staying awake wasn't hard. The girls slept peacefully in their sidecar. Sometime just before noon on the last day we arrived at the designated crossroads just south of Tucson, Arizona.

Chloe saw it first. The *HMS Ophelia* hanging in majestic splendor fifty-feet off the ground. To an eight-year-old girl it must have looked like the flying pirate ship from the end of *Peter Pan*. Actually, it kind of looked like that to me as well. She gasped, and woke her sister, who let out an "OOooo". The two of them started squirming with excitement, since they had been told they were going to live aboard this magnificent flying ship.

We waited in its shadow, as Jean-Paul lowered the hook to hoist the motorcycle and sidecar. As we waited, up lumbered Gyrod. Around his neck was a rope, and on the rope hung one small gear.

"Is that the old one, or the new one?" I asked, nodding to the gear.

"It is the new one," he said. "I was too afraid to remove the old one. I will, when I know nobody is dependent on me. But you need me to guide you into the city to find Father."

The hook interrupted us at that point, as it swung close to our heads. "Watch it!" Jean-Paul warned from above.

I grabbed the hook, looped it around the bike. Soon, bike, girls, and I were hoisted. Up we rose, with Chloe, the eldest girl, getting more and more nervous as Isabella got more and more excited. Finally, we were above the ship's railing, and the small wooden crane swung us onto the deck. There was a crowd of sailors gathered as I unhooked the bike and tossed the rope back over for Gyrod.

Daniel stepped up and said, "What is this?"

"This is Chloe and Isabella." Chloe and Bella smiled up at him. But seeing the sternness on his face, and then looking around at the scarred and dirty faces of the rest of the sailors, they started to look scared.

"Yes," he said. "How long are they staying?" he added in a slow monotone.

"Well, they..." I began, but Kristina then walked up to us.

Upon seeing her, Chloe stepped out of the side car and curtseyed. Then Bella ran to her, and hugged Kristina's legs. That was it, that was all it took. Kristina had that look on her face now, the look of a girl who just found a soon to be put-down kitten at the "humane" society. The kitten mews as if to say, "love me now, or I die". That small hug said all this, and Kristina melted.

Next we hoisted up Gyrod, and he stood stoically over the crew, looking around. He was at least a foot taller than the tallest of us, and all the sailors looked at him reverently. When he finally spotted Timony he strode over to her, and scooped her up in his arms. She giggled like a little girl should when hugged by a big brother – but it was still odd to see, as he was only vaguely human shaped, while she was perhaps *too* human shaped.

That night we sat around the dining room table, discussing what had happened on my trip to find Gyrod, and what needed to happen next. Gyrod and Timony told us with disgust about the cities, and the way they treated their captive population. They told us of their father, a master inventor and craftsman who had been imprisoned in a tower in one of the cities. If anyone could repair our ship, it would be him.

Each city was build like a fortress, walled and well defended. Flying this massive airship over the wall would be suicide. We'd be seen and shot down. The cities were not self-sufficient, however. Huge armored trains came in from all over the countryside, bringing in supplies, and occasionally officials from other cities.

So we planned to jump a train, and ride it into town. Gyrod would accompany me and together we would free his father. In return, hopefully, the scientist would fix our ship.

The "jumping the train" part proved surprisingly easily. Gyrod and I waited in the bushes by a bridge a few miles from the girls' shack. The train had to slow down to cross the old and fragile bridge. As the train lumbered slowly by, we stepped out of the bushes, and climbed aboard. Nobody was inside the one and only passenger car, so we took seats at a table and looked out the window as the train ambled back up to speed on its way into the city.

If I had to guess why it was so easy to jump a train into town it would be this: *nobody wanted into the city.*

THE CHANGE CAGE

The iron giant rattled heavily down the tracks. Every bump was bone-jarring. The view out the window gave a distinct sense of arriving in a land of oppression and control. The beautiful foliage was slowly replaced with dry, cracked mudfields, strewn with rock. It was as if nature itself was staying as far away as possible.

The first thing I saw of the city was immense clouds of black twisting up from a hundred chimneys like huge vines. The sky was darker here, because of the smoke, and I wondered how the emperor justified that pollution.

Then we saw the city. We came over the top of a hill, and for a moment we were looking down at its huge labyrinth of walls. Each city block was contained in a fifty-foot-high wall, creating an uneven grid-like pattern as the blocks stretched out across the city. On top of the walls were roads and tracks, with a few obvious police trains on them, pointing their searchlights into the city below.

In each walled block were buildings, twisted, old and blackened from the coal fires. Some of the 'blocks' were very large, and had hundreds of buildings in them, while others were tiny and crowded, holding just one or two massive tenements. In either case, the walls were high enough that the windows of the buildings either looked at another building, or at the walls themselves, but not a one could view out into the wastelands.

"They keep the people segregated inside the city," Gyrod said. "Each block contains a different race of people, and they aren't allowed to wander from block to block. One block might be Japanese, another Pakistani, another Scottish, et cetera. The theory is that if all those cultures blended, there would be no way to control the cultural and technological advancement. By keeping people segregated, he keeps them from working together, and learning from each other. Segregation is safe storage, if you don't want a people to advance."

"He doesn't want people to advance?" I asked.

"No," Gyrod replied. "He wants to keep everyone as they were in the 1900's. Impoverished, but employed. Unhappy, but controlled. Technology breaks people out of the system. It makes them independent and gives them little need for governments, or corporations."

"These people are slaves to this city, although not all of them see it. They are employed all their waking hours, cogs in a massive, oppressive machine. They are led to believe that they choose the work they do, but in most cases they simply take what's available, and what is available is typically horrible or demeaning, since no one would willingly give up any good position," Gyrod said.

"Since it takes a huge work force to maintain this much control," he went on. "Everyone must work long hours to maintain this life. They work to maintain a life they hate."

I looked back out the window. In the center of the city was one mammoth building, so tall that it thrust its phallic visage into the clouds and disappeared from view. It was huge and foreboding, and although it cast no shadow in the graying dusk, it did seem to darken all around it. There were no lights coming from this building, and no doors or windows to be seen, just a few slotted vents speckling its sides.

"That is the 'Cage', or the 'Box' as the police call it. We nicknamed it the 'Change Cage'. It is a vault, a junkyard, and a prison, and each city has one. Anything that happens in the city that doesn't fit the very narrow definition of what is acceptably Victorian is thrown into the Cage. That includes people. If a man invents something that is too far outside 'acceptable Victorian standards', which typically means anything that's an advancement or improvement, his invention goes in the Cage. If he seems capable of doing this again, he himself will be thrown in the Cage."

"What's in the Cage?" I asked. "Is it a prison? Or maybe just big shredders, like a massive garbage disposal? Or a party filled with all the hippie-outcast-inventors?"

"No one really knows, but you are about to find out. My maker is in the Cage, and we are going in to get him," said Gyrod.

"Then I hope it's not shredders," I said.

The train was now headed down the hillside and across the swampy valley toward the outer wall of the city. The city's feet stood in a vast pool of filth, where sewage and refuse were dumped into the swamps around it. In these surrounding swamps were filthy, sickly giants. The huge gators, hyenadons, and other vicious beasts I had yet to meet all waded in the sewage, looking for anything cast out. From our position on the hill, they looked like roaches and maggots crawling through a rotting carcass.

As we came down the hill, my eyes were drawn to what I thought was a black-domed building. I soon saw the reason my eyes were drawn to it was that it was moving, slowly rising into the night sky. It was not a dome, but a sphere, a huge black balloon, hand sewn, lifting a gondola the size of a shed up and out of the city.

But on the tops of the walls around the city were police trains, and soon their searchlights had fixed on the escaping balloon. They shot long sprays of fire up at it. The jets of fire seemed to miss, and for a few exciting seconds I assumed the fugitives had made it. Then a mild orange glow lit the back of the balloon creating a halo. One of the streams of fire had hit it.

The balloon cleared the wall, but was now losing altitude fast. It suddenly burst, and collapsed, dropping to the ground like a shot. I could see figures leaping from it as it fell, but at that altitude there was no chance of survival. I could only watch in horror as the small figures fell to their death. The police trains then continued on.

Our own train slowed now, and plunged into a dark tunnel in the outer wall. In the tunnel our windows were black, and when we emerged we were shown a bizarre and dismal scene. As if we were on the world's most depressing theme park ride, we slowly passed blackened old buildings, and a depressed populace. Buildings were ornate in design, but so crusted with the filth of coal fires that any beauty in their artistry had been covered. These sat alongside dilapidated, leaning wooden buildings, with crooked walls, and dangling shutters.

There were people everywhere, hurriedly walking through the squalor to whatever dismal jobs awaited them. Instead of the youthful look of the sky people, or the tanned, strong and happy Neobedouins, these people looked tired, and old, with deep frown lines permanently etched on not just the old, but even the relatively young faces.

Even the children worked. From the day they were old enough to hold a broom, some task was assigned to them. I later learned they worked part-time, and went to school part-time, and in that way the adults were nostalgic for their youth: you only worked *part* of the time as a child – the other half was strictly regimented school. I swore to myself I would keep Chloe and Isabella from this life, if I could in any way help it.

The streets were filled with a massive variety of moving things. There were many old bicycles in a variety of sizes and number of wheels. There were steam-powered carriages, buggies with clockwork beasts pulling them, as filthy and depressing as the buildings. There were men on mechanical horses, mechanical ostriches, llamas, or giant armadillos. In all cases, these mechanical creations only looked half-finished. Huge sections of their sides would be missing, exposing the complex gears within. This seemed to be making a statement to any government enforcers who might see them. *This is just old fashioned clockwork! No new technology here!*

In many cases I could even see gears where they didn't belong at all. On the side of a hat, or in the center of a tie, or glued to someone's boot. It was almost as though the occupants of the city used gears as some sort of evidence that they were doing nothing new – nothing progressive. A badge of old-fashioned conformity. These depressed people filled the sidewalks. They wore elaborate but coal-stained garb of red velvet, gold rope epaulettes, corsets, top hats, bowlers, cummerbunds, and bustles. Filthy formal wear seemed to be the city's uniform.

We saw one group of people standing outside a clothing store, engrossed in discussion. "They are likely debating whether the clothing is *really* Victorian," Gyrod said, looking at a cluster of peoples gazing approvingly into a shop window. "Whether it fits Victor's plans of enforced de-evolution. One of their favorite conversation topics is debating if something is truly old-fashioned enough, or what designer or craftsman is about to be Caged for being too modern. If something is deemed 'not *authentic* Victorian', the owner could be cast out, and imprisoned." They have been taught to fear evolution, and so 'in period' for them means maintaining a fashion that hasn't changed in two hundred years. I've seen them report a man for having zippers, since buttons are far more old-fashioned."

He then leaned into the window to glance ahead. "This is where we get off." The train was crawling along now, slowly slipping through a tunnel in one of the massive walls. We stepped past the crates of salvage, and towards the open door. At this crawl, the jump to the ground was easy, and soon we stood on cobblestones between tunnel wall and train, as the massive machine rolled slowly away. We were inside one of the walls that separated the city blocks. As the train's caboose slipped into the tunnel, a massive portcullis-like gate sealed the exit behind it. When the caboose slipped out the other end of the tunnel, a similar gate shut us in.

We weren't trying to get out. Gyrod strode on his long rusty legs to a circular grate in the wall, six-feet wide, and tore it from its hinges and clasp. Then the massive metal man bent over, and stepped inside the round tunnel, and continued down it like a spider in a hose.

Gyrod led me through the tunnel, past a huge fan that had once filled the tunnel but now lay to one side, and on into a large room. In the center of this room was a crate roughly the proportions of a bed. On it lay an automaton, his legs detached and lying next to him. The room was filled with broken pieces of machinery, most of which resembled human anatomy in some way: arms, legs, eyes in an old bucket.

Also in the room was a battered and rusty old man, arms of fine china, legs of iron, who diligently worked with tiny tools on the machine-man who was lying prone on the crate. He looked up briefly when we entered, but upon seeing Gyrod he went back to his work.

"Gyrod, what is our plan?" I asked in hushed tones.

"I'm not sure. It will be tough moving about the streets, as it is clear you are not a Victorian, and I am not at work. Victor's followers are quick to point out anyone who does not fit the rigid laws of the city." Gyrod looked clearly scared. "I would stand out most, as an automaton who is not at work is obviously sentient, and therefore illegal."

"Can we just make a run for it? How do you get into the Change Cage?" I asked.

"The only way I know to get in is by police train. They pass in and out of the Cage all day," he said.

"Couldn't we just allow ourselves to get caught?" I asked.

"Hmm." Gyrod looked concerned. "This troubles me. It seems risky, not knowing our fate once we are inside. But still, the idea has some merit if we do it right."

In the end, we came up with a plan, which honestly, I got from a movie I once saw. You know, that movie where the hero dresses up like a prison guard to break into the prison? Anyway, here is what we did. The police trains travelled on tracks that ran on top of the walls between the city blocks. Throughout the city at various intervals were little police train-stations. When a guard is done with his shift, the small steam trains would stop at a station, and the guard would switch with his replacement. So we waited at the bottom of the steps, and as the exhausted guard came down we clubbed him on the head.

Surprisingly, this doesn't make a man pass out like in the movies. It hurts him, so you club him again, which hurts him more...and then you feel bad, because this is just a guy doing his job and here you are hitting him on the head for no apparent reason.

In the end, Gyrod lifted him off the ground by the back of his suspenders, and I said, "Sorry about this. Tell you what, if you go quietly, I'll make sure you get let out in a couple hours. Make a fuss, and I'll have this seven foot automaton tie your spine in a pretzel. Which will ya have?"

"I'll go quietly, guv'na!" he said. *Oh, great,* I thought, *Not only do they dress these guys like 1890's British 'Bobbies', but he speaks in a faux-British accent, like he's been watching too much Monty Python!* God, I hate fake accents, but I smiled and pretended not to notice.

In a few minutes, another guard came to take this one's place, and this time we skipped the attempt to knock him unconscious, and instead Gyrod lifted him by the throat, as I explained his options to him. He also agreed to cooperate, and I traded clothes with him quickly, and ran up the stairs to the train.

> *I took a steam-train to work,*
>
> *Just like the one my father took.*
>
> *And I pass over the walls.*
>
> *I see the people as I look.*
>
> *- Excerpt from the song*
> *The Change Cage*

I stepped onto the train, leaving Gyrod behind. He would make his own way into the Cage. I entered a car filled with a dozen smartly dressed officers, who turned to look at me in unison, while the biggest said, "You're late. Who the hell are you?"

"I'm...uh...new," I said.

"Ira Nuew?" he said, and he pulled up a clipboard and starting running a fat finger down a list of names. "I've got an 'Ira Chew?'. Is that you? 'Chew', You Chinese? 'cause this ain't block 624 at all!" But just then a bell started ringing adamantly, and all the officers stood up. The train lurched several times, swinging them on their handholds, and finally started chugging down the tracks.

We passed over four walled blocks, before the train came screeching to a halt in the middle of a wall. We all jumped onto a precarious little walkway and ran towards long narrow stairs that led down to the streets.

At the bottom of the steps we came to a man in the street standing between two other officers. "Building Ae14, Floor 12, Home 182. They been handing out homemade remedies for the *black cough,"* the filthy, skinny man said with pride on his face. Obviously, turning in his neighbors filled him with joy.

The large officer from the train took out a billy club and cracked the man heavily on the skull with it. "There's no such thing as black cough, or can't you read?" he said, pointing to a notice posted on the wall. "Michaels, take this man to the *Box* while we deal with these *Progressors*." I remembered the Box was police slang for the Change Cage.

A dozen of us from the train then jogged down the soot-blackened cobblestones until we came to building Ae14. Two officers stayed at the bottom of the stairs, as the rest of us walked quietly up the steps to Floor Twelve. We walked down a rickety wooden walkway to 'Home 182'. The large guard knocked on the door, and said in a fairly convincing falsetto, "Good day, mum. Any remedy for an elderly neighbor?"

The door was opened by a tall, slender, but well-groomed man in his early thirties wearing an apron and small round glasses. "How may I help you, officers?" he asked, looking surprised and scared.

The large bobby gave him a quick glance up and down, and then shoved him aside. He stomped into the living room, and found a series of vials, test tubes, drip lines, and boilers all processing a thin, pale blue liquid. There was a mother and two daughters pressed against the wall of the shabby apartment in fear.

"So why aren't you all at work? The sun is out, and you are all obviously well enough to stand there and cry. I'd say you were well enough to be at work!" our chief said, looking them up and down. He then grabbed the mother by her chestnut hair and pulled her to her knees.

"Wait, wait, I'm the one you want!" said the father, "I'm the one thinking outside the Box!" he pleaded, throwing himself at the chief of police.

"Sure you are," our ruffian said, dragging the screaming crying mother from the apartment. "And that's why you have the hands of a cobbler while her fingers are stained blue. Do I *look* like this is my first day at work?"

The children were screaming and crying now, and as police officers it was our job to hold them back. This was a sore trial for me; helping the bad guy to do bad. As each second elapsed various strategies and outcomes flashed through my mind. But all my ideas lead to the same result; I would be killed and the mother would still be thrown in the Cage. There was nothing I could do.

The chief dragged her screaming back down the cobblestone streets while throngs of her neighbors looked on in horror. Not all of them seemed to disapprove of the police chief's actions, but I did notice that the ones who cheered her defeat all seemed to have a nasty cough.

Back into the train we went, with the screaming mother in

tow. She was thrown in a holding pen so large it required its own train car. They must have often taken dozens of *Progressors* at once in this thing.

The cell they threw her in was not empty. In it were two automatons, one of which was Gyrod, sitting perfectly still, not moving his head or eyes. He looked dead, or vacant, but I knew better. The other was a small girl, with clearly exposed gears on the side of her head where her hair had been ripped out. I sat close enough that I could hear the mother and the small clockwork girl talking in whispered tones.

The girl asked, "Why didn't you leave sooner?"

The mother replied, "To go where? There is nothing out there but death."

The girl said, "But I have heard there is..."

"Sssh!" the mother interrupted, glancing at me with fear.

Soon I could see that ahead our tracks led toward a monolithic building, and as we pulled into the darkness around the Change Cage, I could see the base of it contained a series of train tunnels leading from all over the city.

As the train pulled into the tunnel at a crawl that seemed almost fearful, I heard the captured mother say to the little automated girl, "Whatever you do, don't flinch".

We screeched to a halt on a platform, and the engine let out an obnoxious jet of steam. Two police officers then went into the confinement car on our train, and pulled the terrified woman from the car. Two more officers escorted the automatons out, who went with no resistance, as resisting would show they were self-aware. We were met on the platform by a young military man in a shiny black uniform with silver badges. He held a clipboard, and attached to the clipboard was a small cardboard rectangle.

He said, "Name?"

Nobody spoke, so our piggy-chief smacked the lady hard in the head, "Tell the lieutenant your name!"

"April Adams," she said, clearly terrified and shivering.

The young soldier then said to her in a sugary tone, "Don't carry on so. It's not as bad as all that, provided you are worth something."

"Will I see my children again?"

"Hah! Of course not!" he said, now looking offended. He wrote her name on the card, then spoke again back to the chief, "Focus?"

Our officer replied, "Chemistry. Specifically, Pharmaceutical Chemistry."

The young officer looked at the chief with raised eyebrows through his small round glasses. "My, aren't you specific." His tone was sing-songy, but accusatory.

"I know my job is all," the police chief muttered in a much deflated tone, his eyes on the iron floor.

The young lieutenant already seemed disinterested. "Take her for processing," he said, and two of his subordinates dragged her away as the police officers stayed in line by the train. We were obviously the underlings of the military, and I was getting the feeling we weren't really allowed to wander. That would make this difficult.

On a massive wall I saw a huge signboard that looked like a train schedule. On it was a listing of dozens of disciplines, and under each of these were dozens of names:

Machinery and Magnetism (842):

John Calloway - tasked

Jeff Webber - dispatched

Philip Porter - tasked

Seamstress or Leather Worker (632):

Rachel Fenway - tasked

Thomas Bruin - dispatched

The young lieutenant added to the bottom of a list marked "medical" a card reading:

Amy Adams - Being Tasked

The two automatons walked obediently when told, but the girl's eyes were pivoting quickly around the room. They were led to a large contraption that featured two huge rolling wheels like a rock smasher, each cover in spikes. A conveyor belt lead to this crusher, and as it pulled, huge hammer like weights smashed down onto it. The machine's operator stood the automatons in line by the conveyor, and turned the machine on. There were bits of metal scrap on the belt, and the weights easily flattened them before they were fed into the crusher.

The operator told the small girl to lie on the belt, facing up. She stumbled a bit getting on it, which made the operator raise his eyebrows, but the girl then diligently laid down. The belt pulled her towards the first weight. As it came down she cried out, and leaped from the belt, tripping and falling and breaking on the floor.

"Clearly sentient," the young soldier said, making a note. "Disassemble her!" he said victoriously, and they raised the small child up and threw her, crying and screaming, into the compactor. The manner in which she was crushed would have made a butcher queasy, but being mostly metal none of the soldiers gave her a second glance as her scream garbled and then stopped.

I was shaking with rage at this point, and my eyes were tearing up, but there were at least thirty soldiers and ten police officers in the room. Luckily, it was over before I really knew what was going to happen, otherwise I wouldn't have been able to stop myself. I would have jumped to her aid, and all would have been lost. Still, many a long night since, I have lain awake wondering if I could have helped her.

Next, Gyrod was told to lie on the belt. The first weight fell towards him, but stopped before hitting him as it did with the girl. He lay perfectly still.

"Not sentient. Find out what it does, and we'll put it to work," said the young lieutenant.

"Chew!" said our chief, once again full of boisterous superiority. "You need to get to administration and find out why you weren't on my list," he said this with a growl, but he didn't leave the line of police officers. Instead he jabbed a chubby finger towards a hallway under the sign board.

Perfect! I thought. I stepped out of line, and headed toward the hallway. Just before I stepped into the poorly lit tunnel I read on the wall:

Clock Work Sentience (616)

Down the dreary iron hall I jogged, taking in everything as I ran. I passed what had to be an administrative office. I passed a room full of a hundred different kinds of automatons, sitting perfectly still with eyes unmoving. I passed several hatch doors that led into large vertical tubes. Inside each tube was a platform and a series of buttons, so I assumed these were elevators. I hopped into one, and pushed the button marked "6". The elevator began to rise. At floor six, I stepped out into another hall, this time lined with locked iron doors about fifty feet apart. At each massive iron door there was large lever, and next to each door was a number on a rusty plaque. I ran down past 612, 614 and finally stopped at 616, "Clock Work Sentience".

Gyrod waited by the door, blood on his hands and legs. I had a moment of shock, thinking that whoever he killed might have been undeserving of death. Then I remembered the automaton child's death. To Gyrod, this was reason enough, and my brain whirred in a moral struggle, not knowing if man was allowed to kill machine. But there were more pressing problems.

"Crap," I said. "Now it won't be long before they are on to us!"

"I know. I am sorry," he said, and he looked it.

I pulled the lever by the door, and heard machinery grind and halt. The door was locked.

"Pardon me," Gyrod said, and I stepped aside. With one massive finger he sliced through the iron door like paper. He pulled the door pieces out of the way, and stepped inside.

"Father!" he said, and I heard another voice say, "Gyrod?"

I stepped into the room, and this is what I saw: The room was large, perhaps the size of a basketball court. There were piles of automaton torsos and limbs everywhere. There were tables, tools hanging on cables from the ceiling, and a single bed and chair in the corner.

Standing over an open torso in the middle of the room was a gray-haired man in his mid-sixties, holding small tools he used to select various gears from a tray. As he saw us enter, he set down his tools, and removed the massive pair of goggles that covered most of his face.

"Doctor Calgori!" I exclaimed, for it was in fact my friend the Doctor, looking younger and healthier then I had ever seen him look.

"Yes, that is I," he said in a tired, confused voice. He did not know me.

Now, you must forgive me for tearing up. Although Calgori did not seem to know me, just a few weeks ago I held him in my arms as he died. I strode across the room, wanting to embrace him, but I settled for an enthusiastic handshake as I was clearly a stranger to him. I said, "It's good to meet you again, Merlin!" knowing full well he wouldn't remember his first words to me.

"What? No, I'm....Gyrod, what are you doing here with this *bobby*?" Calgori asked, referring to my uniform.

"I've returned to free you," Gyrod said, "I am so sorry I left, father."

"Nonsense, you had your family to protect. And you came back eventually, so all is good! The plan just took longer than we first thought it might," Calgori said, smiling. Gyrod looked thankful.

"Also," Gyrod spoke. "My friend here needs help."

So I quickly told Calgori about our broken time machine, and the smashed orb. Calgori said, "Yes, I know the style of machine you describe, as I am fairly sure it's based on mine. I arrived here twenty years ago in a balloon with a similar Chrono-adjustment-field-generator. If we could find my machine, we could use parts from it to repair yours..."

But he was interrupted by a gunshot. I turned, and saw Gyrod, a massive pistol at one side of his head, a hole in the other side of his head smoking. His eyes went blank, and he fell with a crash forward into the room. Black-and-silver clad soldiers ran in pointing rifles at us. The young officer with the pistol holstered it, and spoke, "I don't have authority to execute people when they are brought in, but I do have authority when they act such as you have. Take aim!"

"Hold your fire," said an impossibly deep and confident voice. From behind the soldier appeared four men, if they were men. They stood as tall as Gyrod, and were as black as the Africans we sailed with years ago. They were bald, with giant round shoulders and arms, all of which were adorned with symmetrical tattoos of interwoven knotted lines. They had huge curved blades at their waists, and massive gold cuffs on the wrists of their bare arms.

The deep voice spoke again, "These two are being requested by the Emperor himself. Please bring them to the rooftop, and load them into the Imperial Frigate immediately."

The young soldier looked terrified, and responded, "Yes, sir!" Then someone behind me held some sort of sponge to my face, and I blacked out.

BEAUTIFUL DECLINE

Our wrists were in cuffs, and the cuffs were locked to the arms of chairs, but the chairs were very posh. Polished, light tan leather cushions, backs and arms, with gorgeously sculpted aluminum frames. This theme of tan leather and aluminum was carried on throughout this massive cabin; bare rivets hand-bolted brushed aluminum panels to wall and floors, which surrounded the portholes, which were as big as bay windows.

Out this ample view we could see the treetops of a vast jungle, the tallest trees stabbing gold in the early dawn light. Little wisps of morning fog streaked across the leafy jungle canopy, and were so serene and beautiful it was hard to remember our dire position. I couldn't help but think of the harsh and ironic assessment an older Calgori would be making of our surroundings at this time. "Leather?" he would have said, with a disapproving raise of the eyebrow. "The king of the beasts has leather chairs?" This twenty-year-younger Calgori was much more mild than he would become, or at least he could keep his mouth shut better. Calgori's mind seemed elsewhere, probably still working out the geometry of some creature or device he had been building in his lab.

Outside, to our left and right, were smaller, more heavily armed airships. These were the size of the *Ophelia*, and bristling with guns. Not the heavy iron cannon that served us so well, but a variety of more modern weapons; sleek cannon, machine gun turrets, and something that resembled depth charges. This high-tech weaponry was closer to what I might have seen on a warship from my own time.

These crafts had a 1930s flair to them. They were obviously handmade, but made with great skill. They were chrome, aluminum, and rivets in gorgeous sleek lines of luxurious Art Deco. There was nothing Victorian about Victor's personal guard.

Our room was at the front of the massive gondola, I assume one floor below the bridge, so we could see directly in front of the enormous zeppelin. In the distance the pale yellow sun rose over a paler blue coastline, and at this point the jungle cleared to reveal a sprawling, ancient, ruined city. Vines had swallowed these tan-stone Mayan ruins, and huge trees hung over the outer walls. Every one hundred feet around the wall and throughout the city were towers of sculpted steel girders similar in construction to the Eiffel tower, although considerably smaller, and topped with massive copper spheres. At fifteen-second intervals these spheres would simultaneously burst in lighting bolts that, from this distance, looked like a blue web of light in a geometric dome over the ancient ruined city. This array of tesla towers was obviously a deterrent, a shield against airships, should any sky people feel like they wanted an end to the Emperor's reign. I have to say it would be an effective deterrent. I sure as hell wouldn't try to drop my big flammable balloon through this glowing web of lightning!

"Approaching Tulum city," said a crackling female voice over the intercom. I learned much later that Tulum was a Mayan City that had stood on cliffs overlooking the Caribbean Sea since the thirteenth century.

The towers near us stopped flashing just before our airships came within range. They turned off a few towers in the middle, creating a perfect channel down the center for us to fly. It reminded me a bit of an old film, wherein a very Hollywood-handsome Moses parted the Red Sea.

The sky was now pink fading to pale blue, a beautiful Caribbean morning. Over the quiet engines, I could hear the emerald blue surf pounding on the white powder sand. The two airship destroyers held back, as our giant luxury ship slipped silently to the ground. We set down on beautiful grasses, where grazed the greatest variety of flawlessly healthy beasts I had ever seen. Zebra, giraffe, ostrich, llama, tapir, something similar to a giant armadillo, those stupid elelopes that nearly got me killed on the plains, and a hundred other beautiful and exotic beasts strolled through the gorgeously tailored lawns of this ancient city. It was a perfect Eden for a world emperor.

Guards now entered the cabin. They went straight to our chairs, and uncuffed us. "We are very sorry to have locked you up this entire trip, but you would not have come willingly. Please refrain from anything impolite until you have met and spoken with the Emperor. We feel confident that you will not feel the need for violence once you have."

Was this supposed to put me at ease, or creep me out? It mostly did the latter. What was he going to do, hypnotize me?

They walked us down the gangplank to the lush lawn, and at this time I saw a lone figure walking down the massive front steps of what must have been the main palace. I'm not sure what I expected the Emperor to look like, but this was definitely not it. A tall, muscular man in his late forties, tan with sun-bleached hair was walking cheerfully towards us. He was shirtless but wearing a gorgeous black Armani suit of very Twenty-First century styling, and his tan bare feet stepped lightly from the old stone steps of the palace to the lush green grass of the lawns. Had he been younger, he could have easily been a model, but now his deep smile lines and crow's feet gave him the look of a very attractive movie star nearing an early retirement.

He had a huge smile, sparkling green eyes, and he jogged up to me enthusiastically. "I am so very, *very* glad to meet you!" he said with genuine enthusiasm, as he grabbed my hand and shook it. "I have dreamed of meeting you for years, and hoped you would one day step into my time! Hopefully, I can set your mind at ease quickly, so that we may spend many days comfortably exchanging stories from our travels."

I stared at him, perplexed. "Okay. My name is Robert." The Emperor smiled at my name as if telling him my name was a clever joke. I continued, "Nice to meet you." This felt like make-believe, but I was going through the motions to see what would happen next. "Oh, and this is Doctor Calgori?" This last I said more as a question, since it was growing apparent he knew very well who we were. As I introduced Calgori, I could see the doctor's face glowing red with rage. He had obviously seen too much of the oppression of the cities to have his forgiveness bought with a pleasant smile from a charismatic man. But if the Emperor noticed his anger, he didn't show it.

"Come with me to breakfast, and we will talk! I will answer all your questions, in exchange for a few good stories from your travels, and thus we will spend a wonderful day together!"

Not seeing many options, since there were massive, turbaned Imperial guards everywhere, and starting to feel a bit peckish, I followed him across the lawn toward the beach. Between the ruined, vine-covered temples were gorgeous, huge topiaries. All kinds of beasts, both real, extinct, and imaginary, had been rendered in these beautiful gardens, and among them strode the very real menagerie, looking just as fanciful.

There were also two large mausoleums of much newer construction than the city around us. Over the door of each were the names Emperor Victor Joseph Hippocrates the First, and Emperor Victor Joseph Hippocrates the Second. The Emperor turned to me and smiled. "A ruse, of course. It's always been me throughout the years, as I'm sure you've now guessed. I travel back and forward through time setting plans in motion to create this Eden you have been enjoying. Much like yourselves!" he added with a smile.

"Eden!" Calgori growled under his furrowed brow, but the Emperor either did not hear or chose to ignore him.

"I didn't want my people to think me some strange immortal creature," the Emperor continued. "So I have faked my death several times, and posed as my own son and now grandson as needed. I chose this city because it has been unchanged since the thirteenth century. If you wanted to make your home in a place that would never change, no matter what time you traveled to, this is an excellent spot. Very clever of me," he said with a sparkle which meant that he wanted us to know he was joking when he patted himself on the back.

"I had furniture constructed of the highest, most long-lasting quality and placed it here long ago. Now my rooms stay nearly unchanged no matter what time I travel to!" He grinned smugly. "Of course, if you travel too far back in time you have to deal with the city's previous occupants, as I once learned. Not a pretty bunch, those Mayans, I barely survived the meeting. Still, it gives me nearly a thousand years to work with, and believe me, you can accomplish a lot with a thousand years of non-linear time to play back and forth in. I have staff in most eras of the last few centuries, and they await my appearance to take my commands and execute them."

As we walked, the palace and the sea were to our right, and to our left I could see a massive and gorgeously adorned hot air balloon being inflated. The gondola was sitting on a pedestal between topiaries, and attached to it was one of the glass orbs from the *Ophelia's* Chrononautilus! On the side of the gondola was an anchor and spool. This was obviously how the Emperor managed his time travel–he'd go up in the balloon, jump through time, drop anchor and descend to nearly the same location but in a new era.

Soon the grass ended, and we stepped onto beautiful white powdered sand. Waves gently rolled onto the beach, and sleepily slipped back into the vast blue sea. In the middle of the sand was a tent of luxuriously ornate fabric, with decorative posts, golden ropes, and flags depicting the symbol of a deer eating a growing leaf. The sides of this tent were tapestries, and the scenes on them ranged from wildlife to what might have been illustrations from the *Kama Sutra*'s more advanced pages.

The Emperor turned back to us with a sly grin. "This will be a pleasure for us both! Allow me to introduce you to my wives!" We came around to the front of the tent, which was open to the sea. Inside was dark, but we could see silhouetted on the translucent cloth walls a huge bed on which were the almost pornographically shapely silhouettes of two women. They embraced and were kneeling on the bed between numerous tasseled pillows, kissing. When they noticed us, one of them leaped from the bed and ran to the Emperor. She was more flawless than a fashion model in her barely existent bikini and terra-cotta tanned skin. She looked at the Emperor doe-eyed, threw her arms around him and kissed him deeply.

When they had finished, he said, "This is the lovely Flora." He took one of her hands off his shoulders and held it out to me to shake. She took my hand in her tiny one, and shook it without taking her eyes from the Emperor.

"Pleased to meet you," I said. She said nothing, and her ice-blue eyes seemed to judge me unworthy of their gaze.

"Flora, now say hello to the Doctor. Without him, your wonderful life could never have been this luxurious," said the Emperor, so Flora turned to him and said, "Then I thank you sincerely, Doctor." She said this in a way that told us that she not only throughly enjoyed her life, but also throughly deserved it, and that she in no way truly credited the Doctor for her successful placement in Eden.

Then the other silhouette in the tent stood up, and with a slower, more purposeful stride walked toward the threshhold. Even before I could see her features, her pace and body language told me this was a woman, not a girl like Flora, and she was powerful and capable of great wrath.

The Emperor spoke again, "And here is my first wife, Fauna. Fauna is actually a nickname, as you will see. You know her by another name." Out from the shadow of the tent into the bright morning sunlight stepped Lilith Tess.

Lilith was no longer a young child barely out of her teens, filled with an unquenchable desire to be noticed. This Lilith was a woman in her mid-thirties. She walked with authority, and power. In her eyes was a fire I could not begin to guess the cause of. "It is good to see you again, Captain," she said in an even tone that sounded neither sincere nor sarcastic. She glanced at the red rings the hand cuffs had left on me, and said with a slightly victorious smile, "May I assume your trip was comfortable?"

"Lilith!" was all I said. I was flabbergasted. You'll recognize the emotion; have you ever been having a really bad day, everything seeming to go against you, and right at the end of it, when you felt at your very lowest, you ran into your ex? That's how I felt.

The last time I saw her, she was a young thing who had kissed me, been rejected, and run away embarrassed. Here she was, walking to me out of her palatial porno, Empress of the world? I think I may have been bested.

Flora still had her arms around Victor's neck, but as Lilith walked to us he pulled them gently off. He strode over to Lilith to kiss her, but she turned her head at the last second, and all he met was her cheek. She did not make eye contact with him.

"I trust you two have had an enjoyable morning?" he asked her.

"Yes, we have," said Lilith with a touch of poison and victory in her tone, and she pulled away from him.

"I am glad!" he said undaunted, "Then let's have our breakfast, and let's catch up! Fauna, are you pleased to see your old friend?"

"My name is Lilith," she said as much to herself as anyone else. "And yes, I am pleased. Captain, tell me what you've been up to. More fruitless heroics, no doubt?"

"Well, yeah. So it would seem," I said.

A few yards away, servants were bringing a large table to the sand. They placed it with some care to make sure it was level, and others brought tablecloths, chargers, plates of fruit, bowls, pitchers and bottles of Champagne. We sat around this white-painted table on white-painted chairs, and the servants placed the food on our plates, except for Lilith, who placed her own. The servants kept their distance from her as she gave off an aura of wrath.

"Oh, for Christ's sake this is too damn much!" Calgori blurted out. "There are eight-year-old children employed all their waking hours in order to live a filthy life and eat scrap, while you sit here eating fresh fruit from every continent, at a beachside castle! People in the cities are dying, killing themselves just for a chance to escape, while you have orgies on the beach? While five-year-olds are stolen from their desert cribs and eaten, you play here smug and happy in your domination! You killed millions of people to get here!"

Flora stood up and shouted back, "You stupid pitiful ugly old man! Do you know who you are talking to?" Her face was red with indignation.

"Sit down, my love," said Victor calmly, but his voice had changed from enthusiastic host to an almost terrifyingly powerful man. "I assure you, you are mistaken, Doctor." His large strong hands were spread out on the table before him, as if his will was flowing out through them.

"I am no such thing!" said Calgori. "In your cities, walled into the filthy holes you allow them, the last of humankind rots imprisoned! If they try to escape, you hunt them down, just as you slaughtered man to near extinction over the last two hundred years!"

"HUMANKIND!? MANKIND!? You tiny-minded, idiosyncratic fool! You have mastered the minuscule intricacies of clockwork and chemistry, but you cannot see anything larger then your own infectious race! I have mastered this planet. I alone have restored balance to this globe, and you say, 'Slaughter'!? I saved the world!"

He stood now. "Oh, the vanity of your race! You would kill all other life on this planet for your own good, and call it progress! Other species die off by the billions, and trillions, to make room for your roads, suburbs, cities, airports, and shopping malls, yet you continue to breed, build and fester in war, pollution and death.

"Don't blame me for the filth of the cities," he went on. "That is *your* precious human race, and its inability to stay at a balanced capacity in any given biosphere. Don't blame me for the hard lives you give yourself. Don't blame me for your pestilence, and misery. You brought that on yourself millennia before I started fixing this human infestation."

"I am not the Emperor and Custodian of *Mankind*," and he said this word with disgust. "I am the caretaker of the world! All things, plants, animals, even stones and rivers and the seas have a peaceful purpose. But all these are spoiled and soiled by your precious *Mankind*. This world has a balancing point, and humans are incapable of sticking to it. There is a proper number of all things, and all things stay to their proper numbers until your *Mankind* interferes."

He pointed to a slice of orange that had fallen into the sand when the servants had brought the food. It was now covered with ants, and the trail of ants led up to the grass. "This earth is a perfect system. It cleans itself, and takes care of itself. When fruit drops, it will be eaten by beast. What beast can't eat will be removed by insect. What insect can't finish will be cleaned by bacteria. Even the foulness of Man will be wiped clean in a few years, if the amount of these pollutants can be controlled. Leave a house, and in a surprisingly short time, trees will consume it, vines, desert sands, or the sea will wipe it clean and leave the earth perfect again."

There was a statue on the beach, a dark-green copper Buddha, thick with patina, brought no doubt from Cambodia for the royals' amusement. The Emperor gestured to it, and his rant began to slow into a rhythmical rhyme, more like he was remembering poetry then inventing it on the spot.

"Fingers of rust gently intertwine, and lace the seams of

sacrifice in beautiful decline. Catalyst of creation, of all that was Mankind, pull our corruption toward nature, the state is predefined. All that floats upon the sea, all that hangs in the air, all that sits in dust or dirt, eventually ensnared. The gentle touch of time will take you unaware. Pulling all creations down: an elegant affair. Pleasant patina pulls apart a holy copper shrine. Like gently creeping mossy claws, scarring all divine. All the things you think you value, including the gift of life, will slowly, gently fall apart, until the world is right."

"But by your hand hundreds of millions have died!" Doctor Calgori stood up now, himself full of wrath.

"NO! Not by *my* hands!" Victor yelled back.

"Then by your will, by your orders!"

Now Victor looked pained. "This is not true!" he said, sounding less certain. "All creatures that die in nature die at the jaws or claws or talons of someone else. I rebalanced nature, and I did so in the most natural of ways!"

"By leading men, women and children to slaughter?" Doctor Calgori asked.

"I had no part in that. I gave orders to rebalance the ratio of men to beasts, and when I reemerged a few decades later they had been followed and that phase was successful and over. It may seem gruesome to you, since you choose to view things from your one small human perspective, but your kind has been herding and executing its prey for thousands of years, and in far less kind and fair ways." His speech was growing calmer now. "Do I need to tell you about the slaughterhouses, and the chicken factories? Could you possibly remain naïve to what your kind had done for so long to all the other species on this planet? And how much worse it would be if you were to continue your horrific growth? I have done no more than restore a balanced population. And now I do no more than maintain that, and prevent mankind from regrowing."

He stood quiet, thinking. Then he began again, "I do not pretend to oversee the inner workings of every city. I do not make the choices for all the small decisions made by my Admirals, and Governors, and Mayors. My mind is on the global picture. Let the little people see to their little issues."

By the end of this he seemed to have satisfied himself. He tossed his napkin onto his chair and stomped up the sand towards his castle. Flora, too, left the table in a huff, and Calgori and myself sat silently for a minute at the table with Lilith. She glared at the two as they left.

THE EMPERORS WIVES

Doctor Calgori was agitated himself, and walked silently down the beach, leaving me and Lilith alone. We'd been talking with the Emperor all day now, and the sun was beginning to set.

Finally, Lilith broke the silence. "He can be wrathful," she said, in an almost apologetic tone, "...but he has accomplished great things at great cost, in the face of the nearly assured destruction of the world. Come, let me show you around the castle, and I will explain everything."

We walked up the beach, and into the palace. Inside, it was both lavish and ancient. It was more like a castle preserved for tourists then a lived-in home. The decor was opulent, and exotic, as if the luxuries of a hundred nations all provided their greatest treasures for this one abode. Sculptures from Greece, China, and Indonesia posed proudly in alcoves or in the center of rooms. Long leather riveted sofas from Italy sat invitingly on deep and ornate carpets from Turkey. There were many huge globes, mechanical orreries, telescopes, and ornate screens of carved teak. There were chandeliers of intricate brass, inlaid with a thousand facets of colored glass.

There were cats lying on every chair, with lush colorful fur. These cats were flawlessly clean and healthy. There were also birdcages of the most amazingly ornate designs, with many floors and rooms, sculpted elaborately of dark metals. In them were a vast variety of birds, most of which I had never seen before. These cages were perfectly clean, or being cleaned as we passed them, by small, quiet, brown-skinned women. The doors of these cages were always open and the birds flew in and out at will.

The cats and birds seemed an odd mix, and I did occasionally see the cats stalking the birds. Nobody did anything to stop this. Perhaps this game of survival was part of Victor's attraction to mixing these incompatible species? Was this a game of balance he played with himself? Where most homes might have a chess board laying about, Victor instead had a small ecosystem fighting for their lives? Entertainment at the cost of lives, not merely pets.

Yet the most distinctive things in the palace of the Emperor were the calendars. They were massive, many yards wide in thick carved frames. Each calendar spanned not a month or year, but an era, illustrated by hand, in gorgeous detail. By walking the halls of the Emperor's palace you could easily see all the eras of humanity. Some of these calendars were old, but some of them were very newly drawn, and some had huge sections crossed out with a massive red line. Was Victor planning more changes? Planning to simply remove events from history? He must have often commissioned artists to redraw these calendars constantly – or perhaps as he changed the time line these simply changed to reflect it, drawn by artists who lived their long lives in the new time lines he created. These were the kind of thoughts that could keep you up at night.

It seemed grotesque to me to see his changes laid out so purposefully. He would simply erase political movements, governments, or peoples as he saw fit. Erasing the past to create the future he wanted repulsed me – until I realized that's exactly what we had been doing with the *Ophelia*. And we had been doing it with much less care and craftsmanship. We just haphazardly removed events we generally thought of as "bad", with no thought to the consequences. Victor was "gaming" the history of the planet, reshaping all that had ever occurred, in an effort to build his perfect world. Realizing this made me feel shallow and short-sighted.

As we walked, Lilith talked with a quiet urgency. It felt like a confession, as if I was to absolve her of the story as it unfolded.

"When I met him, he lived in a time where the cities had grown so large that their edges connected. It was horrible, and he was young, handsome, brilliant and tortured on behalf of this planet he loves so dearly. Together we created this plan to restore balance. It was his passion, not mine, but I supported him and worked with him."

"Wait, I'm confused," I said. "All politics aside for a second, how *did* you meet him, Lilith?"

"It was long ago now, ten, twelve years I think? It's so hard to remember accurately with all our travel," she said, getting a far-off look in her eye. "I had talked Tanner into helping me steal a part of the Chrononautilus – not the whole thing mind you, just a small part you wouldn't miss. He said he couldn't see the harm in me striking out on my own, and that I deserved it. I wasn't getting the attention I deserved onboard the *Ophelia*. Tanner was easy to manipulate, he always has to make everyone happy! His greatest weakness was his unquenchable need to placate everyone."

My face flashed hot and red, and I could feel my pulse in my cheeks. How many of our crew died that day because of this selfishness of Lilith's? This might have been twelve years ago for her, so she could refer to it matter-of-factly, but this betrayal was only a few months past for me. I bit my tongue. If I lost my temper now I would never hear her story, and (setting aside any religious beliefs you might have) this is arguably the most important story ever told.

Lilith went on, "I also took your Chronofax, and I must admit that has proved far more valuable than I would have guessed at the time. When it went missing, we lost a great tool," and then a look of worry flashed across her face.

"Anyway, Tanner helped me take the plans from Calgori's

cabinets," she went on. "And remove the parts from your ship, all while assuring me it would do no damage. I think he was reassuring himself, mostly, as I hardly cared about your damned ship and crew. You ignored me."

"Lilith, I had to ignore you. I *couldn't* give you the kind of attention you wanted..." I said, but she went on to prevent that topic from coming up.

"I spent a year reassembling the Chrononautilus, and I made a small craft that was just big enough to take me up out of harm's way, and into what I assumed was a brighter, richer future. My goals were small then, I just wanted back to the life I saw in your time, making music with all those people fawning over me. I wanted what you had; to be the center of attention. But when I arrived in 'the future', I found a world of concrete, and filth, and angry machines driven by an angry population. It was nothing like I had imagined it.

"I nearly died that night, falling thousands of feet into a lake as my balloon was severed the moment I traveled. Victor found me, and pulled me from the water. He saved my life!"

She went on, "He was young, rich, beautiful, and tortured by the greed of his parents. They spent their life tearing down nature to build this ugly new world, and he was tormented with the guilt of it.

"He was in graduate school, learning all he could about the natural world; environmental science, farming, political science. He vowed to undo the destruction of his family, and was arming himself with every discipline necessary to do it. When he learned of the Chrononautilus, he immediately saw its potential. So together we laid a plan to use it to restore balance to the world. We planned and studied, and all the while we fell deeply in love."

By now we had wandered most of the castle, and found ourselves again on the beach. The sky was now deep crimson at the horizon, and purple high above, as the sun had recently set over the castle and jungle. The sand was firm under our feet where the waves had wet it.

Lilith spoke with longing for these days of her life gone by. "Our first travel took us back to the great Depression. The land was held in famine, and disease. Victor had an education decades more advanced then this era, and he used it to fix these problems. After he did, political success was easy."

"Complete political domination was also guaranteed, thanks to you," Lilith added with a poisoned smile.

"Me? What the hell did I have to do with this?" I said skeptically, and a little insulted. "And why would the people of the world let you do these things? Why would they let him change the laws? Why would they let him unify the nations of the world? Surely they saw how well that worked for the British Empire! And for Nazis, taking towns full of people off to be killed. Didn't anyone remember the Holocaust? How did nobody see this coming?"

She continued with a wicked grin, "But those things never happened. Not from their perspective. With all your heroics, you were changing history, and the world was becoming dependent on you, and naive. Anytime something truly bad was going to happen, you snuffed it out. By the time Victor started his campaigns for World Emperor, there were really no historical warnings for the people of the world. Having one ruler just sounded like a convenient simplification to them," and she laughed.

I was stunned. Mankind had no way of seeing this coming, and it was my fault.

Then Lilith continued more slowly. Something was troubling her memories. "But Victor was obsessed, and he took many more trips then I. This caused him to age three times as fast as me, since he would spend so many years away accomplishing his plans." Her eyes were moist, now, and she went on slower, "Then one day he returned..." And she inhaled sharply. "With her!" In her eyes I saw fear. "At first it was a shock, and it felt like betrayal, but he said it was not. She was for *us,* not him, he said. I did not fully believe him, but I was curious, so I pretended I did."

"We were young, Flora and I, and obsessed with our own beauty. This new love was exciting, and it was taboo, and indulgent, and wonderful! And horrible, and hateful, all at the same time. But I had his attention again – this was something new I could do to get him excited about me again," she said this as tears started to swell in her eyes.

"He brought her here to this palace on the beach, and here she stays lavished in luxury. We work, him more than me, I will admit. I age while I work by his side, but all the while she sleeps here on this beach forever young and beautiful when we return."

"At first she was our indulgence together. While she indulged herself in our opulent success, and we indulged ourselves in this taboo love."

Now her eyes went wild. "But it all went wrong! Have you seen? Have you seen how she looks at him!? She loves him, and he her!" She was growing wrathful, now, as we stood on the beach. Her eyes burned with anger, fear, jealousy, lust, love and hate. Tears and fire. It was a toxic mix of fuels, and it surged dangerously in her.

"He asked me if we wanted to leave her, but I couldn't bring myself to do it!" she said exasperatedly, desperate, like an addict talking about an addiction. "He asked me if I wanted to leave him with her, just us girls together and he alone, but I loved him and couldn't! I am also not sure she appealed enough to me without him there to hold my interest – part of the thrill was the attention I was getting from him for this. I want her love, and his, but I did not want them to love each other! So I asked him to leave her, but leave her to only me. He agreed, and he agreed to not tell her, for she would never, ever forgive me if she knew I took him away from her." She was panicking now with this mix of guilt and anger and jealousy. "And so he tells me he pretends for her benefit, but I think he is pretending for *my* benefit!"

Then her eyes went wide, and she screamed angrily, "*Look at them!*" She was looking up toward the palace. There, through the sheer curtains of the royal bedroom, fluttering in a sultry evening breeze were the flawless figures of a man and woman embraced. The woman's back arched gracefully, and she threw back her long hair as he kissed her chest. Lilith screamed, "They lie! I knew!!" And she ran toward the palace.

I realized I hadn't seen Calgori all afternoon, and I quickly scanned the beach for him, but couldn't see him. Lilith was at a lower entrance to the castle now, and I knew nothing good could come of her storming in with her wrath, so I dashed after her.

Up the beach I ran, vaguely aware of the sound of propellers. I entered the castle, and in the dark I stumbled upon stairs. It was hot and the air felt stagnant and moist, but filled with urgency.

At the top of the stairs there were two imperial guards, with their massive tanned arms, uniform tattoos, and dark red turbans. "No guests in the Harem," one said in an impossibly deep voice as he blocked me. I swear I could hear strange, inhuman yelling coming from the grounds outside the castle, and the guards must have heard it too. They seemed distracted, but stayed at their posts. As their attention was on this sound, Lilith passed the guards to the royal chambers slowly and methodically. Only I saw that just past one of them, she slipped a lithe hand into his belt and removed his massive knife. She disappeared into the room.

I then heard a young woman scream, and a man wailed, "My love...!" but he was cut off before he could say more. The guards turned and we ran down the halls together into the chamber.

In a room of white silk, three bodies floated like *Ophelia*, facedown in a river of blood.

I would eventually write these lyrics:

> *The Emperor's Wives*
> *In a deep dark forest kingdom*
> *Under Banyan covered skies,*
> *Lived a king with untold riches;*
> *Jewels, gold, and two fair wives.*
> *Every night he indulged his fantasies,*
> *enjoyed his wives, and went to sleep.*
> *As he slept his wives kept secrets,*
> *holding hands under the sheets.*
> *Each dark day in his ancient palace,*
> *The Emperor sat on his throne of gold*
> *while his young wives explored bright gardens,*
> *eyes met eyes and hands did hold.*
> *One bright day in the dead of summer*
> *a pretty young wife saw a look of love*

on her lover's face towards their husband
fires burned jealous; she'd lost her love.
One hot night in the dead of summer
the Emperor's wife stole a magi's blade
crept into her lover's chamber,
and as they slept her lovers she slayed.

THE WRATH OF FATE

We stood in this palatial room of white, in astonished horror, the guards and I. These deaths changed so much about the world that we were briefly immobilized, with no clue what our next move should be.

When I realized that this new turn of events wouldn't likely change my incarceration without a little personal liberation, I began to back slowly away from the circle of guards. Just at that moment, the door of the room filled with armed soldiers. They wore the black and silver of the Imperial Navy. The last man who entered was powerfully calm. He had a white beard and huge bushy black eyebrows, and he wore the uniform of a Grand Admiral.

Walking straight to the nearest guard, he growled, "Due to the *unforeseen* death of the Emperor." Had he said *unforeseen* ironically? "I am assuming command. You are hereby relieved of duty. You will be taken to trial, and then punished for the death of the Emperor Victor Joseph the Third." The soldiers placed the Imperial Guards and me in restraints.

"I've survived the Change Cage once already," I said boldly, while thinking, *Why am I talking!? Shut up!*

"I find Cages inefficient means of removing filth from the population," he snarled back. "You will be tried, found guilty, and executed. Before dawn."

Soldiers took me and the guards outside, where we found a military airship in a yard littered with the bodies of the Emperor's menagerie and many of his guards. Zebra, giraffe, gazelle, and a hundred other beautiful beasts lay dead amongst the Emperor's sentinels. *How could they have had time to do all this, let alone know about the Emperor's death, and be here at this exact moment?* I wondered. Then it occurred to me. *The Chronofax!* If he had access to it, he could send himself a message of the

Emperor's death after it had occurred! He would then have his soldiers in place at the exact time of Victor's death!

Our cuffs were latched to an iron fence, as the air frigate lowered its boarding ramps. As I stood chained and at gunpoint, it struck me that two things did not make sense. First, the tesla towers were not flashing. They must have been disabled for the Admiral's frigate. The second thing was that I was hearing propellers, but the frigate's props were not turning.

Then I heard a massive *Ploom*, and saw familiar shockwaves ripple across the gas bag of the frigate! The warship was taking fire! *Ploom, Ploom!* I heard again, and one of the shots punctured the bag and it began to deflate.

Most of the soldiers now ran away from their airship, firing rifles into the red-black evening sky. Only three riflemen remained to guard us. I noted the point of impact on the frigate's gas bag, and turned in the direction the shot had come from. The *Ophelia* was cresting the top of the palace! In she swept, sideways from the sea, broadsides blazing!

The Admiral strode out of the palace in a rage shouting orders. As he came past us, he said, "Kill the prisoners. To hell with politics, this is my reign, now!"

The three infantry men turned their guns on the first three of the Imperial Guards, and fired. It happened so fast, there was no time to do anything. The shots hit the massive guards square in the chest, and none of them flinched.

"Reload!" yelled their sergeant, as they slid back the rifle bolts. "Aim for the head. Ready, aim, fire!" And this time the massive imperial guards fell limply forward, faces burst open. They swung head down, hanging from their cuffs on the fence.

I, and the other two guards began to pull at our chains, and kick at the fence, as the sergeant again yelled, "Reload!" When loaded, they turned the guns back towards us. The reality of the situation seemed clear. I stood in a field of dead, chained to a fence with the dead. I thought my fate was sealed.

The sergeant yelled again, and with rifle barrels so close I could smell the powder, I heard "Ready! Aim!"

But before he could yell "fire!" I hear a familiar sound overhead, *Screeeee-chika-chika-chika-chika!!!* Our captors looked up to see a seven-foot brass man fall amongst them. Gyrod swung his bar twice, and the soldiers folded in horrific ways and flew across the grass.

Then with an easy pinch of two fingers, Gyrod crushed the chains between our cuffs. "Follow me, Captain," he said in his comfortingly familiar, rasping voice. There was a large hole in the side of his head, but he seemed fine.

"How are you alive!?!" I asked in wonder.

"Oh, Father didn't put anything too important up there. When I was shot in the Cage, I just pretended," he said.

The *Ophelia* had dropped altitude, and her underside crow's nest was nearing the ground. I motioned for the recently unemployed Imperial Guard to follow, and the massive hulks of men ran with Gyrod and myself towards my ship. *My ship - I need to never leave her again!* I thought.

The crowsnest was now in the grass before us, as the enormous ship was skillfully piloted from overhead. Whoever was at the wheel was much more precise than I was! Gyrod, the guards and I leapt in and immediately the ground fell away as the massive vessel lifted into the air. The sea stretched out in front of us beyond the palace, and I knew I would be glad to see the last of this twisted center of a dying world.

But a second later, we heard a massive "Crack!" as the tesla towers fired in unison. This flash of wickedly precise lighting lit the scene of chaos below us as it set our beloved *Ophelia* on fire!

We climbed the rigging as the ship came about, and headed out to sea, but as we climbed, the thick wooden planking of *Ophelia's* underbelly was burning horrifically, and ropes fell around us in a shower of ash.

Luckily, the rope ladders spread to the outer rails as they went up, so we could, in theory, get on deck without having to contend with the fire. But the heat from the fire of *Ophelia's* underside was setting our rigging ablaze. One of the Imperial Guards' ropes burnt through, and he fell ten feet before being caught by Gyrod. He was lucky the Automaton was there, as few men could have stopped the fall of such a massive hulk as he.

The lower mast holding the crow's nest burned through, and as it fell it pulled our rigging taut with a snap. This nearly shot us from it like a slingshot, but we held.

Behind us a dozen massive warships were clearing the tesla array.

We climbed the rigging in the nick of time. In fact, I saw the lower mast and crow's nest fall free as I climbed over the rail.

On deck I saw perhaps the most horrific sight of my life. Most of the crew lay charred on the deck, bodies burning, while the sails and airbag above us was covered in flames. It was like a scene from Dante's Inferno, everything was ablaze, and I recognized some of my friends burning on the deck around me. We had been lucky down on the crow's nest – the teslas had hit deck level at full force.

I ran to the helm where Daniel barely stood clinging to the wheel. His clothes were burned, still burning in spots. He was pulling desperately on the inclinometer. I joined him, and together we spun it futilely. The *Ophelia* was starting to fall.

Then we heard a whistling sound from behind us, and I glanced back to see a volley of airborne missiles impact our gas bag! A series of two dozen explosions sequentially incinerated it. The aft deck was now swallowed in flames, and our sails and gas bag flapped, deflated, like the last flag of a defeated revolution.

And then we fell.

Down we plunged; A fiery ball, a skeletal frame of ash.

With air bags burst at three thousand feet, all our hopes were dashed.

Nothing could keep airship aloft, so down we crashed.

Five hundred fathoms down we fell, towards briny deep we splashed!

~ Excerpt from the song The Wrath Of Fate.

The *Ophelia* fell like a brick, and charred bodies lifted into the air as she did. Daniel and I held the wheel now just to stay aboard, there was no hope in steering.

We hit.

Our ship, as massive as a six-story building, hit the ocean with the force of a three-thousand-foot drop. It slammed into the ocean like it was hitting a wall of stone. Water cracked timbers, and ashen bodies bounced and broke on the deck like ceramic dolls.

At the exact moment we hit, there was a massive burst of pink smoke from the side of the ship as each Chrononautilus orb burst from our impact with the sea. This cloud spread at an unrealistic speed across the deck and up into the sky. Whatever it hit it froze in mid-air. Men snapped to a halt mid-leap, bodies froze horrifically in the air, swinging ropes and lanterns locked at unnatural angles, and fire froze in place.

The pink clouds then turned to gray, and we were in a thick fog, still frozen in place. As I hung there, upside down, I could see Daniel's shoulder was badly burned, and his face was too covered in ash to gauge. Being that still and dirty, he looked inhuman. Dead. My only clue that he was still alive was that his hands still grasped the wheel. I could see other bodies in pieces, or burning.

Then an overwhelming sense of horror brought pain to my face and chest. Where was Kristina? Where were the children? If they were below deck, they would be crushed by this impact. Above deck, and they would be among these charred bodies. The thought wrenched my chest from the inside – this thought was the worst pain I had endured all day.

Slowly, the fog started to lift, and the things on deck dropped. As time began to slowly creep forward, massive waves rose up around us like walls. Finally, all motion snapped back to full speed, and the walls of water crashed around us, engulfing the deck, and crew, the *Ophelia*, and myself.

As suddenly as the waves had swallowed us, they released

us, and withdrew. I could not sit up, but with one hand I brushed water from my face, and looked around. The deck was washed clean, and the fires were completely quenched. There was nothing above us now, no gas bag. Only stars.

"Thank god the kids weren't onboard for that!" said Daniel. And I went limp with relief and laid back, drenched with warm salt water.

I stayed there for only a second, looking at the stars, when the stars were interrupted by large, black, growing shapes. Things were falling. Soon, the severed fuselages of six massive steel warships plummeted through the sky and plunged one by one into the sea around us, and the sea swallowed them wholly as they hit.

When our Chrononautilus burst, time had been frozen in a huge sphere around us, and the rest of the world kept moving. The wrath of fate is wicked, and as fate would have it the edge of this field fell midship in the attacking armada, severing them.

The *Ophelia* started her life as a sailing ship, and her wooden hull had survived the impact of the waves. It now held us afloat. But the steel fuselages of the naval frigates were heavy, and not water tight. The ocean swallowed them and never let them go.

We slept where we lay, too wounded and exhausted to move. The warm ocean rocked us gently in a way that was reminiscent of the way the *Ophelia* had swung on her rigging. I woke from time to time and stared at the moon.

Finally, I opened my eyes to a pink-golden dawn. As the sun rose slowly over the Caribbean Sea, Daniel and I walked slowly around the deck, taking inventory of who had survived.

Gyrod was there, and nearly unblemished. In fact, during the night while we were collapsed, or lay dying, he went silently around deck pulling crew out of immediate danger, or nursing those he knew how to help. He was now sitting next to a large chest he had pulled up from below deck, and was trying desperately to dry himself with cloth from it, for fear of rust.

The two Imperial Guards had survived, although one had massive burns to his face and shoulders, and the other had one eye that would never open again.

And speaking of cyclopses, Mongrel had been so drunk below deck that the impact had left him fairly uninjured, although his smell hinted that he had been sick on himself. This might have happened before the fall, however, knowing him.

Timony, the little clockwork doll was there as well. Much of her skin had been burnt off, and she was terribly broken, but she could still speak. Hopefully, she could be fixed.

Calgori had been picked up down the beach while Lilith and I talked. He'd been below deck during the fall. When he saw the deck and sails set ablaze, he warned as much of the crew as he could, and then managed to stow himself in a sea chest of uniforms before we fell. Jean Paul pulled him alive, but unconscious, from the box and carried him on deck. When he woke he looked and moved much like the older Calgori I had known.

We saw no more of the Grand Admiral's Navy that month. My guess is he had seven ships at Tulum City. The *Ophelia* had incapacitated the first as they rescued me, and the final six were severed as the *Ophelia* fell into the seas. It would take the Admiral himself a good long time to get to any Naval bases he might have, and that bought us our escape.

"Gyrod," I asked, thinking. "What is that you are drying yourself with?"

Gyrod stood, and pulled yard after yard of white canvas from the massive sea chest, looking at it questioningly.

Mongrel stepped up and, holding his head in one hand he said, "Wha' on god's earth is that gold'n man doing with the spare sails???"

I looked at the sails, and then looked up at the mast. When the *Ophelia* had been retrofitted for air travel, the mast had been left intact. During all our travels, it stood up through the airbag, aiding the lanyards in holding our ship aloft. It towered above us, charred, but strong. This ship that had once been a sailing ship, would be a sailing ship again! At least until we were able to get her aloft. It was time to rebuild her, and to raise sail.

"So where next?" I asked the small gathering on deck.

"We best not go ashore," said one of the Imperial Guards. "Least ways, not for a while. I say we head north east, and try to come across one of the flotillas of the Sea Gypsies. They'll help us repair and set things right."

"And we'll need to get word to Kristina and the girls," said Daniel. "Tanner is keeping an eye on them in Isla Aether. It's a little mountaintop Skyland in the Rockies. Beautiful place. The docks stretch out into the skies, and the whole town sits in a sea of clouds like an island in the sky."

"Something still needs to be done about the three Change Cage Cities," said Calgori. He had slowly woken now, and was listening.

The Emperor was dead, and the world was free from his Mankind-hating agenda. It's hard to judge a man who had accomplished so much for the sake of the world. Mankind had paid a dear price for the world's salvation, perhaps too dear a price, but the world had been saved.

It came down to scars and scabs. The Emperor had deep scars because of the guilt he felt for the actions of his family. That drove him to vast accomplishments. I myself had scars from my childhood, and a need to be important, a need to be strong and heroic. This, too, drove me to making a huge impact on the world and its history. In doing so, I and my crew had *removed* the scars of Mankind. That weakened us as a race, and allowed Victor to take over. I think scars are necessary—without them there is no strength.

Now the Emperor was dead, and in the Emperor's place a new tyrant had risen. This new tyrant is perhaps the true villain of the story, since it would appear that it was he who executed the most reputedly villainous plots in the Emperor's name. Perhaps the Emperor had never given the orders to kill, but mearly asked for balance and turned his head away while his Grand Admiral did the killing. I'm afraid I don't know the full story of Lilith and Victor, but maybe there will be a book one day to tell it.

We drifted off into the sunset, not knowing what we'd meet on the seas, or if they contained beasts as vicious and hungry as the ones on land. We didn't know if we'd get back into the skies, and we were too tired to be concerned about what happened next.

The only thing left to do was to make sure Doctor Calgori got into the Emperor's old balloon and traveled back to the 1880s. After our fall, his memory was starting to fail him. Hopefully, he would have the mental resources to create the Chrononautilus. I was sure he could.

...but today's story has been told.

THE END